# MAGICAL W

# MAGICAL
# WOMEN

Stories edited by
Sukanya Venkatraghavan

First published in 2019 by Hachette India
(Registered name: Hachette Book Publishing India Pvt. Ltd)
An Hachette UK company
www.hachetteindia.com

SRD

ISBN 978-93-88322-02-7


Hachette Book Publishing India Pvt. Ltd
4th & 5th Floors, Corporate Centre
Plot No. 94, Sector 44, Gurugram - 122003, India

Typeset in 12/15 Venetian 301 BT
by Manmohan Kumar, Delhi

Printed and bound in India
by Manipal Technologies Limited, Manipal

'*May we never be held hostage by old narratives…*'

AMRUTA PATIL, *Manifesto of the Uncowed*

# CONTENTS

# EDITOR'S NOTE

**W**hy should *Magical Women* exist? Because we need stories that feel like us, sound like us, wear our skin, celebrate our features and, most significantly, flaunt the magic that is so uniquely in our blood. We need to tell these tales embedded in our culture and imagination, about the magic we have forgotten we possess, or are told we don't, because the world is afraid of a female who knows she is powerful.

Each story in this collection is unique in its representation of what it means to be magical. For some of the characters it is a natural part of who they are, like the courtesan in Shreya Ila Anasuya's 'Gul', or the goddesses in both Trisha Das's 'Tridevi Turbulence' and Krishna Udayasankar's 'Apocalyptica' – magic as a familiar aspect of divinity as is shown in our own mythology or folk tales. Others, like the lone survivor of an accident in Ruchika Roy's 'The Gatekeeper's Intern', discover their power and learn to trust and wield it. The protagonists in both Nikita Deshpande's 'The Girl Who Haunted Death' and Shveta Thakrar's 'The Carnival at the Edge of the Worlds' look to question and reshape their origin stories. Kiran Manral's dystopian tale 'Stone Cold' speaks of magic both ancient and modern that will thrive under any circumstance. Are we always comfortable with our innate witchery is a question Shweta Taneja's 'Grandma Garam's Kitty Party' asks, and Samhita Arni's 'The Demon Hunter's Dilemma' is about choices in a magical world. Tashan Mehta's 'Rulebook for Creating a Universe' is a fine example of how feminine sorcery has always been feared by the world and the time-hopping protagonist in Asma Kazi's 'Bahameen' gives a sense of frenzied magic, one that cannot always be controlled. Magic channelled as a form of rage is evident in Sejal Mehta's 'Earth and Evolution Walk into a Bar...', S.V. Sujatha's 'Gandaberunda' and my own 'The Rakshasi's Rose Garden'.

Each story is original and stands for a collective secret power that threads the writers together. These storytellers have been inspired by our own rich tales of women who are ready to subvert their fairytales, find new stories and retell the old myths from our vast South Asian heritage. I am proud to present this diverse constellation of stories – heartbreaking, uplifting, joyful, funny and surreal all at once. You may or may not have heard of them before, but they will feel familiar, because these are narratives that have been running through our blood since the dawn of time. To create this universe of stories and have you read them is a dream come true. These are our stories. You may find your own among them.

Sukanya Venkatraghavan

# GUL

## SHREYA ILA ANASUYA

'A woman in the shape of a monster
a monster in the shape of a woman
the skies are full of them.'

— Adrienne Rich

The halls of this vast house are windy. There are domed lamps and carpets woven to dizzying intricacy covering every inch of the floor. Honoured guests recline on bolsters, the scent of jasmine wafting on their expensive wrists, fragrant blossoms that are theirs for the taking. But take it from this old courtesan. There are unseen women everywhere, though you will not know them even if I tell you their true names. Step into the shadows, and there they are, filling the halls.

Women who knew how to arch an eyebrow or make a bawdy remark at just the right moment, or laugh wildly, just as they pleased. Expert musicians of their time, breathtaking poets, dancers who could put any master of yours to shame. I know these women, I knew them.

Of them, only very few survived the bloody tides of the Mutiny and its aftermath. The old order, in which they had had a place, perhaps sometimes a precarious and strange one, but a place nonetheless, collapsed entirely. Begum Hazrat Mahal's unending war ended. Lucknow fell, and the pale ghosts who arrived to plunder this land bit down on its jugular. All our patrons and paramours scattered; many were hanged, many more exiled. That was the moment the axis of our world shifted – and precisely because it was pivotal and bloody, it is the moment they recount the most. Lucknow of 1858.

But what is far more brutal is the slow passing of time – what the pale ghosts started, the good people of this land made sure to finish. People of high standing, wearing crisp cotton woven by hand, lovers of music and culture all – people who couldn't move a finger without walking on the backs of those who washed their fine clothes and scrubbed their inherited mansions clean. They wrung our necks; they smiled as they did it. Over the next few decades, those of us who would not, or could not afford to hide our origins were pushed, pushed, pushed – whirling away from the centre of the mehfil to the corners, where most of us lingered, where our daughters linger, where their daughters will linger until the last one perishes.

Some of us survived it. Some through marriage, some by hiding our true names, some by becoming safe embodiments of the very world that had been destroyed. I, Munni Begum, survived by doing all of this. This is how you still hear my voice, echoing at you from the years that stretch between us. This is the plain truth – I am among a handful who were lucky.

And then there was Gulbadan.

She arrived one morning at Zeenat Bai's establishment. I was nineteen then and had been performing for a few years.

She wouldn't tell us where she came from, but that was par for the course for us. She was no girl, but time had not left its mark on her face in the way it criss-crosses most faces. It only became a kind of knowing that never left her eyes, even when her moon-face was twisted in peals of laughter.

She had exquisite, long fingers, and a perfectly straight back. She held her body with the ease and grace of a dancer. Her voice was low – honeyed when it needed to be and rumbling when the situation demanded, breaking and circling and echoing through our usual repertoire of songs that were either about love or worship, or often about both at the same time. Ghazal, thumri, qawwali – she could sing it all with ease, locking eyes with each person in the audience so that, for a moment, they felt like the only person in the world.

It was this quality that quickly made her one of the most fêted tawaifs in Chowk. It was not simply that she was considered beautiful or that she could be perfectly charming; there was something else about Gul that made people of all kinds throw themselves in her path.

I saw nawabs blush when she winked at them during a performance, sigh when she seemed to consider them lovingly for a minute and then turn away, her eyes flashing like the diamond in her nose. In a matter of three months she was adding more to Zeenat Bai's coffers than could have been expected of any new entrant to the house.

There, I have told you the public version. It is no secret. Anyone who was alive then and knew her will tell you as much. That she was skilful. That she was magnetic. That she was a mistress of her arts.

But what nobody knows about her is that she was my Gul.

I was besotted with her. She could tilt her head at me and I would trace the arch of her eyebrows in my head for nights afterward. She made me feel impossibly tender. If we were simply lounging together early in the evening, the sound of her smoke-filled voice would have me tracing circles on my thigh.

She knew it, of course, though she feigned not knowing at first. I could not have hidden it from her for all my trying. I tried hard, embarrassed at the force of my own passion, confused by the heavy presence of her in my breath, in all my days. She had reached out and taken my heart in her fist, simply, easily, just by standing before me one morning.

I suppose I should not have been surprised that she crushed it just as easily when she fled in the suffocating days following the end of the Mutiny. This is after she had lifted my chin one evening in the middle of me reciting a foolish ghazal I had written in her honour and made my heart leap to my throat when she kissed me softly. I could not believe she loved me back, and never fully trusted that she did, although she insisted as much to me in hushed whispers when we awoke entwined some mornings, or by way of thrilling notes that she passed to me even as we hurried to change our finery in the middle of crowded performances.

Her love was lush, it is true, but it was entirely on her terms.

She chose the nights I could spend in her chambers, and this I did not mind. What I did mind was the way she dismissed our relationship in front of the other girls in the house. This was by no means the first time in Zeenat Bai's house that two women had fallen in love. But because of Gul's magnetism, her popularity, the way so many of the men who came to our salons were as besotted with her as I, the household's acceptance of our relationship was hesitant. About this she did absolutely nothing; there was no sign in front of them of the ardour she displayed when we were alone together.

She remained icily silent when my eyes filled with tears if she took a lover from among our patrons. But when I tried to rebel by taking up with Samina, my age-mate and equal in the household, Gul's retaliation was swift and unforgiving. Her anger was always reserved solely for me, and only behind the closed doors of her room. There she become something else, my moon-faced Gul, when she showed her teeth to me in a way that had nothing to do with smiling. The one dark spot high on her bronze cheek, her eyes the colour of burning coal, her waist-length raven hair, her dark lips full – all this seemed to melt away in that moment, and the enchantment of her face became of a fiercer, wilder quality. I was in love with her; I was terrified of her. Fear and love became locked in a fierce embrace, and fed each other like air feeds fire.

But then a different, more menacing fear gripped our entire household. The pale ghosts introduced a rifle that required equipment that was greased with the fat of both cows and pigs. An entire regiment refused to bite the cartridge and was punished mercilessly for not obeying orders. That is when, you can say, our troubles began, for many of the plans for the long months of rebellion that followed were hatched in our very salons.

Those months were subdued; the air itself felt oppressive. We had fewer performances, and when we did the mehfils were not as joyful as they had once naturally been. With more time on our hands, Gul and I started shopping for the household ourselves. Sometimes we took Zeenat Bai's only son, Karim, with us to help us haul our bags home. Karim's birth, unlike his sisters', had not been celebrated, nor had he been as extensively educated as them, so he earned his keep by running errands for the house and making sure our books were kept in order.

On the day before I was to turn twenty, Gul insisted she wanted to make me some kheer, and we went to buy the ingredients – thick, fresh milk, fragrant saffron and raisins. Karim came along, and the three of us were in good humour after what felt like aeons. Gul was wearing a simple embroidered kurta of white, and as usual her diamond pin flashed on her face. To this day when I think of her, it is this image of this Gul that comes to me – fresh-faced, light, laughing easily.

Perhaps this was the final moment of my innocence, the final blossoming of the years in which I had spent so much time immersed in reading and writing, understanding music and dance, learning how to converse and compose. It was a light that a darkening world cannot bear, especially on the faces of women, especially on the faces of women such as I. Perhaps someone cast an evil eye upon us. Perhaps I was too happy, despite the fact that things were crumbling around us, and I had no right to be. Perhaps I loved her too much.

For at that very next moment Gul caught the eye of a Lal Kurti. The officer stopped us with a glint in his eye, which travelled to his mouth and became a smirk as he looked at Gul from head to toe. My blood curdled. I wanted to tear his eyes off her, and I was about to say something. She knew me so well that she sensed it, and put a steadying hand on me. Karim, beside me, seemed struck silent with fear. I had never felt so humiliated.

Then he spoke, in the kind of accent we had mocked hundreds of times. 'How much for a turn with you, girl?'

I started forward, but Gul pushed me back. I whirled to look at her. In the entire year I had spent with her, I had never seen the kind of cold fury that overtook her face then.

'What did you say to me?' She spoke in a voice I did not know. It boomed with the power of a thousand more, echoes within echoes.

My stomach felt cold as ice. For a few seconds the market seemed to cease its jostling around us.

Then, as suddenly as it had seemed to be sucked out of the world, the clamour came back. I saw the soldier's face tighten, but he didn't seem to be startled, like I was. 'Don't waste my time, girl. I know you are one of those nautch girls. Don't make me haul you off.'

She had arranged her face into a too-radiant smile. I knew this face well, she used it with particularly cloying patrons, who wanted to hang around too long after the mehfil was officially over. 'Come with me, sahib, my rooms are just around the corner.'

I stared at her, but they were off already. I watched them for a few seconds before I ran after them. She glanced back and shot me a look. *Stand back*, it said. *I know what I'm doing.*

When she emerged from the alley she had led him into a mere handful of minutes later, it was by herself. She refused to say a word to me all the way home, while I cried silent tears of rage and confusion. The fear had returned in full force – though she said nothing, and scarcely even looked at me – and it was here to stay, for the next morning, she had disappeared.

We had spent the night together, but she had said she would much rather speak the next morning. I usually awoke if she did, but that night I had felt unusually laden with sleep – when we finally slept – and did not stir. When I woke up to the first rays of the sun filtering through her gauze curtains, I noticed that I was alone. The cream bed sheets lay rumpled, her satin-wrapped pillow abandoned. I thought she had gone to wash her face, and stretched while I waited for her, anxious to discuss what had passed the day before.

Some strands of her impossibly thick hair lay scattered upon her lightly embroidered pillow. They made me think of our lovemaking the night before, how forceful we both had been, different from the languorous nights I had come to expect from our time together, nights I savoured. But the night before had left a tight knot of desire in me still, I wanted more of her — and the unanswered questions from the market only made me more restless. As the light outside intensified, I grew more and more nervous, and still she did not return.

She did not return.

By midday, the household began to hum with questions. By then I had searched everywhere, every room, every balcony, every terrace. I had run out of the gates, madly, tears streaming down my face, and Zeenat Bai had to restrain me. I had punched Karim when he tried to placate me, and I had refused to stop screaming her name until they shut me in her room. They did not do it unkindly, nor was I left alone — Samina was there with me, but nothing would console me.

I was sure she was in danger. Perhaps the soldier had returned in the cover of the night and taken her. Perhaps even now she lay dead in an alley somewhere. My moon-faced Gul would never have left me on purpose, I knew. She had been taken, and had I been allowed to leave the house I would have scoured the city for her, looked in every street and corner until I found her and brought her back to me.

And then, in the afternoon, just as I had fallen into an exhausted stupor, the doors of her rooms were flung open and I came face to face with three Lal Kurtis. 'Where is she? Gulbadan?'

Before they could stop me I ran out to the main halls, where more Lal Kurtis were stationed. Zeenat Bai was sitting on the floor, coolly, gurgling at her hookah. The man Plowden, their captain and our sometime patron, was questioning her. Strange to see him here, after so many months – he had attended many of our mujras, and his wife, Lucy, had had a special fondness for Gul. She had even asked Gul for lessons.

Zeenat Bai wore a tight smile on her face. 'I do not know where she is, sahib, she has abandoned the hearth that fed her for a year. She is as faithless as a wild cat.' Zeenat Bai was nothing if not astute. I knew that most of her valuables and our money had already been spirited away, just enough remained in the house that they could take. I was hopeful then, thinking she herself had stowed Gul away somewhere. But in a second, she said something that dashed my hopes. 'And I'm well rid of her, for I will have no murderer in my house.'

I shrieked then, and she started. 'Shut up, you foolish lovesick girl. Your precious Gul seems to have killed a soldier that she was seen talking to in the market yesterday. They found him in an alley this morning, not a single mark on him, dead as a block of wood. Lord knows in what dark arts she dealt, to be able to do this... She has left all of us here to rot, you included. Pull yourself together, or get out of my sight.'

I do not know how I spent the next weeks, months, year. At first I refused to perform, and they let me be. I kept vigil by her windows, by sunlight, moonlight and candlelight. I scarcely ate or slept. I cried until the tears ran dry, and when I could no longer cry I read poetry she had written through swollen eyes. In my head I heard her sing, a monsoon dadra about dark clouds gathering, a woman tormented by the absence of her lover. I felt myself floating out of my body, and from my vantage point near the ceiling I saw the thing I had become, hollow-eyed, my hair unwashed and in knots, my lips dry. I had become the absence of Gul.

After a few months Zeenat Bai herself started coming to feed me. She called the munshi to read me poetry, she dragged me to see the other girls rehearse for mehfils. Soon, she began pestering me to sing again, lamenting, screaming that all that education had been wasted on me, that I was not the first girl to be betrayed by a lover, that my name would forever be lost if I did not come to my senses.

I had begun to feel other sensations slowly, and this included a considerable degree of guilt, for I had contributed nothing to the household income for over six months. I began to sing again, though I still could not bring myself to dance. I sang with lowered eyes. But my voice, when it emerged again after a few days of careful riyaz, surprised me. I had been a competent enough singer before, my training substantial enough and my delight in poetry genuine, so that I could sing convincingly.

This voice, though, was different — richer, deeper, unwavering and immense as though it was coming from somewhere else. Had I always contained this ability and, obsessed with my love for Gul, never noticed it? Or had she, by leaving me — for I knew by then that she had deliberately left me — made me into the singer I had become? I do not know, except that now when I sang about longing I felt it in my bones, when I sang about the fecklessness of a lover I understood the words, and the bylanes and alleyways of the music itself, like I never had before. Betrayal had enriched my voice, and anger, when it gathered, fuelled my riyaz, so that I began to sing more and more, better and better, each raag I learned and each thumri I mastered an answer to Gul's desertion.

And that is the voice you now know, if you know your music. The voice that took me in the following decades of my life to the Delhi Durbar to sing before King George, the voice by which I made a fortune for myself, setting up my own establishment at the passing of Zeenat Bai, and eventually buying property all over the city even as many of the women I had grown up surrounded by faded into obscurity. As they retreated to the shadows, pursued by lectures on morality and demonized as being unclean, I took my spot in the light. And as I prospered, my heart crumbled.

I met and married a devastatingly beautiful businessman, Irfan Ali Khan, and became Munni Begum. His family disdained me and threatened to disown him. For a time, I was forced to give up music, but through that time he loved me truly, and could not bear to see me with my face tightened in agony as I watched others, always others, perform. Much quarreling and cajoling later, his family decided that I could sing anywhere in the country, as long as I sang nowhere I could sully their good name. And so I took off to Benaras, to Rampur, to Calcutta, with Karim acting as my manager, and a handful of young pupils in tow.

It is not that I did not love again. I was very fond of my husband, I enjoyed his gentleness, his fine mind. I liked making love to him. But I never loved him I like I had loved Gul, and if our partnership lacked the inconsistency and ultimate cruelty of the one I had shared with her, it also never matched its life-giving fire. Now, what set my pulse dancing was singing, and teaching the young girls whose training I had been entrusted with. To them I was all, they called me their mother and followed me where I went. The older ones, in some years, started accompanying me on stage.

Eventually, long after my body died, they would be celebrated, honours conferred upon them by famous men. But even as their greatness would be lauded, they would always be known as pupils of the great Munni Begum. Some would write books about their years with me, and one or two would sing forever like me, never finding that precious and irreplaceable thing – the power of their own voices. The more successful ones would train many pupils of their own, and one would start a school in my name, established in my honour. For I would become what only a handful of humans become through what they leave in their wake – immortal.

But you've read this script. Greatness, true greatness, is only conferred upon the crone. As maiden and grown woman, whispers followed me, and even as my career arced upward like a meteor, it would be years before my considerable donations to the freedom movement would even be acknowledged. I was old when they came to love me simply for my music, for by that time my origins and my story became two different things.

In one's sixth decade, it is difficult to stay angry. What fire I had in my belly I reserved for music, for the push and pull of the taan, for the trick and love affair of singing two exquisite lines of poetry in three different and expansive ways. I had outlived my husband for ten years already, and had immersed myself in caring for my pupils. Still, what artist with some ambition remaining can resist the lure of the capital? Younger women than I were thronging to Calcutta, playing parts on the stage, at the big theatres – Star, Minerva, Classic. Some of them had been dancers, some could sing.

The capital called to me, the same pale ghosts who had so tormented us during the Mutiny were soliciting women of my talents to sing for a new contraption that had been created, for which a man called Gaisberg was meeting with gaanewalis both young and experienced.

It was called the gramophone player, a golden creature with a gaping flower for a head and a box at its tail. This is how you sang for it – you not only had to scream into the blasted cylinder that snatched at your voice, you had to hurry it up. A lingering thumri would not do – you had to squeeze the song, with all of its pathos and play, into less than one-third of the time you would otherwise have had with it. And, when you were done, you had to tell the machine your name, or they would not know who on earth you were.

We had taken some rooms in the Great Eastern Hotel, and it was there that Gaisberg had set up his little studio. Every day I spied the young girls going in and emerging. Gaisberg's assistant, a reedy Bengali man named Sen, had approached us – but even though we were there, Karim remained sceptical.

'I don't know, Muniya…I heard some strange things about this machine… Let's wait and see,' he told me.

'Like what? Don't tell me this is like that time those men came to photograph me?' I teased. All these years of working and living with me, and my poor Karim still struggled with naiveté. It went back to our upbringing – so differently were we brought up in the same house and by the same woman. My affection for him strengthened rather than waned because of this.

'Muniya, I am serious. Someone from Janki Bai's party told me that the machine…it traps bits of your soul into it everytime it catches your voice. It may be best to stay away.' I began to laugh, and he knew he had already lost the fight. After this, I decided to not push the gramophone issue too much with him; I knew I could make him come around in a few days. I could do what I pleased, but he was my oldest friend, and I did not like to frighten him.

*The Bengalee* had a review of a new show in town, played by a tremendous new actress called Elokeshi, and Zoha, my oldest pupil, had cajoled Karim to take us to the Star that evening to see her play Janabai.

The theatre that evening was absolutely packed. I had dressed in one of my favourite sarees and put my hair up carefully into a bun, but in the quiet hush of the theatre just before the show, everyone's eyes, including my own, were turned towards the stage. I heard the soft creak of one of the doors being opened, and turned around in some irritation. I should not have paid it much mind but something kept my eyes on the figure that slid quietly inside. She was simply dressed, almost nondescript, but when she passed me, I recognized her with a start, with a pain in my heart that is impossible to capture in words.

The only person I had known my entire life who could have captured it with her song was now looking directly at me, as surely as she had looked at me when I was only nineteen. Gulbadan.

And she looked exactly as she did then – how was this possible? And how was it possible that no one else noticed her, not even Karim, seated beside me? They seemed as frozen as I, but nobody had their eyes on her.

As though she was putting on a private performance meant only for me, the woman I had known as Gulbadan transformed before my very eyes. Her limbs looked somehow more supple, her hair grew longer and more lustrous, her face suddenly – terrifyingly – sharper. Her clothes changed, became a mendicant's, her forehead suddenly marked with a little ash. And almost as though she had always been there, she was onstage, and everyone around me broke into applause.

That evening Gul – Elokeshi – gave the best performance I had seen her give. It would be a surprise if audiences forever after did not call her Jana. There was a standing ovation at the end, and she was called back on stage by the audience's cheers – she returned, bowed, disappeared.

My heart hammering, I turned to Karim, who had not recognized her at all. How could he? He had only been allowed to see her terrible beauty, the face of Elokeshi.

I did not say a word to him. I spent the night awake, as I had once lain awake thinking about her after she had left decades before. But now I began to see how she could have been so clairvoyant. Her little tricks. Her great skills. Her overwhelming fame. Her ability to slip away at will. Her face, teeth bared, monstrous in anger.

She was not just a keeper of lore. She was part of its very fabric.

The next day I told Karim I had an evening appointment with Gaisberg and went back to the theatre. I watched her again. I was certain she knew I was there. And acting upon my certainty, I went backstage. I told an attendant to let her know Muniya was here to see her. In a matter of minutes, I was inside her dressing room.

Her hair was long, loose. Her moon-face full, not a day older than she had looked when I was so much younger. Her eyebrows arched darkly on her forehead. She smiled; her face shifted, she made herself, again, the Gul of old.

'How are you, my love?' She was smiling in an old way, a way that wrenched my heart when I first met her...a way that she knew, I could see, still worked.

'Gul…'

'I owe you an apology, my darling, and an explanation. But I am afraid I am only able to give you one of these things. Please accept my sincerest apologies. I should not have left you like that.' She was calm, perfectly calm, calm in a way that frightened me even more.

'What I saw last night…that was you? What were you doing? What…'

'What am I? Only cloud and water, my love. I am Elokeshi on the Bengali stage. I was Mah Laqa in Hyderabad, and a long time ago, I was called Amrapali. In the coming years I will have more names and faces. The calamities are not over for our kind, my darling one. I am so glad you made a name for yourself. It will carry you far.'

'I have so much to ask you. So much to tell. Come with me, spend some time with me.'

'I wish I could have stayed, Muniya…'

I knew then she meant to leave me again. For the first time in many years, I felt an old resentment swell up inside me.

'Why do you do this?' I asked. 'Play with a little human life?'

She turned to me then, eyes flashing. If she was capable of hurt, I had managed to hurt her. I felt a tiny whiff of satisfaction. 'I never played with you. Never. It gets exhausting, watching people die. It is better to go when you get too close… My love, it was good to see you again.'

With that, she opened the dressing room door, and was almost borne away by the crowd that thronged outside. It called her name, 'Elokeshi!', and wanted to swallow her up. She paused, turned. Her face was different again – tinged with softness. I saw an old fire in her eyes, older than me, older than time, a fire by which I had warmed myself in the time we had had together, and without knowing it, for years after.

We looked at one another for a long moment. Then she spoke again, this time with a new urgency. 'Listen, there is something called the gramophone now, it can copy your beautiful voice for people in another time. You must record as soon as you can.'

What was this? I could not fathom why she wanted to now

focus on something so inconsequential. 'I intend to, Karim doesn't trust the machine, says he hears strange things about it.'

'What, that it captures a little bit of your soul and keeps it trapped inside it forever?' She laughed then, the same wolfish laugh that undid me as though I were still a waif of nineteen, the same fear gripping my insides as though it had never gone away. 'It's true, my love. It's all true. And that is why you must do it. Do it.' She opened the door, stepped away.

I stood there alone, blinking in the sudden light.

\*\*\*

Bombay, 1995

Amol is hooked, he can't help it. He's at Sagar Bar every night with his buddies, after a day of running around collecting for their bosses, occasionally beating up the shopkeepers and business owners who won't pay up. The work is exciting and the money is easy, and how better to spend it than see moon-faced Rosy every night?

Raju and Guru are in the mood to heckle him tonight. 'What, took your girl to Apsara Theatre again yesterday? What were you doing? Watching the picture, or something else?'

Bastards. They love their dancers too. Raju is even seeing one of the girls, Meena. Besides, Rosy doesn't let him touch her. He doesn't much care. Being with her every evening — being the man who gets to do that — this is somehow enough. He isn't used to this...this feeling. Is this what all the film songs are about?

Just look at her. The most famous dancer in the joint, men throw thousands and thousands of rupees at her in the course of one night. And why shouldn't they? Look at her whirling, her skirts aglow, the silver moons embroidered on them gleaming. She is dancing to an old ghazal, something about thousands of men driven mad by her eyes. When she dances like that, when she smiles like that and looks at him, he feels like the only man in the room.

Afterwards, he is impatient to go home. She is not one to be pushed, so he waits — what else is he going to do? He watches even as Raju and Guru leave with their girlfriends. Finally, she emerges, dressed in a simple white kurta.

'Rosy, *jaan*, I've got something for you. Come, let's go to your rooms, *na*.'

She is indulgent today. The season's first rains have begun. She had once told him monsoon was her favourite season.

In her rooms, with the gauzy curtains and the old-fashioned lamps, he proudly pulls the disc out of a slim bag. It has the flat, round face of an old singer on it — it looks impossibly old, like it belongs to a different world. 'Munni Begum — Classic Hits! See, huh?' He is delighted, nervous. He doesn't quite understand this music himself, but he knows she likes it.

The rain starts to fall gently outside, and inside they let the little needle fall on the black disc, which turns and turns. The song is about dark clouds gathering, a woman looking for her lover. Rosy closes her eyes and throws her head back. He feels a rush of love overcome him. When she opens her dark eyes he thinks he can see pinpricks of tears in them. She smiles. 'It's gorgeous,' she whispers.

In the flickering light, the diamond in her nose glints, and you could be forgiven for thinking that her face changes ever so slightly.

# GANDABERUNDA

## S.V. SUJATHA

'*Gandaberunda*.'

I pulled down the elastic waistline of my skirt and bent over so he could see. On my lower back, it would be: a bird with a gigantic body and two heads, the faces like that of hawks, eyes watchful and feral and filled with shades of fire, plumage blazing golden, talons long and curved like blades, dripping scarlet blood. A bird of prey. Swooping, wings spread, on the brink of attack.

His fingers were on my bare skin, the smooth manicured nails tracing the tattoo. He let his touch linger there for a few moments, caressing, and I let him. 'That's some weird shit,' he finally announced.

'You're weird shit, motherfucker,' she growled. The ball-sized tumour above my pelvic bone was throbbing. Thump, thump, thump, it rang, her angry, impatient heart from within. Buried under layers of cloth, skin, fat and muscle, yet deafening. I knew he couldn't hear her, but I was still unnerved. I straightened up hastily, my skirt snapping back into place.

'Is that all? Or will I find more art hidden away in interesting places?' He was staring at my thighs, my crotch. He grinned when I met his bloodshot eyes. He was filling up our glasses again. I downed my drink in one hard gulp, gagging a little as I swallowed, the cold beer frothing against my tongue, dribbling down my chin.

'Wow. You do drink like a fish, Amaya. You weren't lying in your Tinder bio,' he cackled. I flashed him a coy look, then pulled out a red lace handkerchief from my handbag and wiped my mouth. 'No, I wasn't. I'm an artist, and I like getting inked and travelling and watching Tarantino movies. I eat like a bear, sleep like a dog, drink like a fish.' I remembered what I had written. It was mostly true.

'An artist? You sell your stuff in galleries?'

'I do graphic design for print ads.'

He smiled. A thin, condescending smile. 'Doesn't sound like it pays much.'

I smiled back. 'I get by, somehow.'

He nodded absently, already losing interest in the conversation. 'You know, Amaya, let me get you something fancy to drink. Beer is for peasants and football fans,' he guffawed. He got up, swaying drunkenly, wincing as he stubbed his toe on the coffee table. He stumbled across the room to the wine cabinet then returned with a bottle and two sparkling wine glasses. 'Merlot. I save this for special nights, like this one,' he purred, flopping down beside me on the couch, popping open the cork. He wrapped a hand around my waist and gave it a slow squeeze. 'I am so glad you came over. We're going to have so much fun, Amaya.'

'We sure will, *behenchod*,' she snapped. I draped a nonchalant hand over the tumour. The flesh near my pelvis was getting hot. Her heart was beating quicker, louder. This was getting distracting.

'So, where do you work?' I asked. I already knew. I had done my research: he owned a chain of jewellery stores in Tamil Nadu and was an official distributor for Rolex watches; he lived in a mansion on Boat Club Road; he used this condo only to throw private parties or bring over girls for date nights; he drove a Bentley; he owned two vacation homes in the US.

'I work with Appa,' he mumbled. 'How is the wine, Amaya? I bought it in Napa Valley last month.'

'Excellent,' I said, as I took a long sip. It was too sweet.

'I knew you'd enjoy it,' he said smugly. 'You can't afford this on an artist's salary, can you?'

His words were already slurring. While he finished his glass, he spoke about his wine collection and stroked my Gandaberunda tattoo like it were a cat. Soon his hand slid up, under my shirt, fumbling with my bra strap.

'No,' I said, pulling away. 'No. Not yet.' He stared at me dumbfounded, blinking, apparently confused by my rejection. I picked up my handbag and got to my feet, but before I could take a step away, he had yanked me back onto the couch.

He moved in so close his breath was in my face. Fruity, rotten and hot. 'You're not leaving. Not until we fuck,' he declared. He moved quickly and deftly for a drunken man. He had me pinned under him within moments. His tongue crawled into my ear like an errant reptile. 'I'm not wasting my Merlot on a tease, you stupid bitch. Now spread your legs and take it.'

'Let me out, let me out, let me out!' she screamed.

The lump above my pelvic bone was blistering, smoldering, as if on fire. I was afraid it might burn a hole through my skirt. I was surprised he couldn't feel it. Her heart was striking against my skin like a furious hammer, again and again and again, pleading and demanding.

'It's time,' she insisted. 'Let me out!' She was all I could hear.

'Okay, let's get this over with,' I whispered, to her.

He grinned. He thought I had spoken to him. He relaxed his hold on me and reached down to unbutton his pants. 'Trust me, you'll like it.'

I closed my eyes as I lay back.

Then I let Anani come out.

It was her turn now.

***

It was time.

Amaya's eyes grew wider. They were no longer black, but had turned a pale grey, the colour of rain. Her cheeks filled out, suddenly fuller and tinged with a soft pink glow, and her jaw widened, but only slightly. Her nose became longer, more aquiline, the tip curving into a slight hook. Her lips folded in like origami paper, making the shape of a heart. Her hair grew long and thick, curling at the edges like burnt paper. The curves and pockets of her face filled with more flesh, rounding off the sharp edges. She changed swiftly, within moments, her features shifting and moving like sand.

And then, just like that, Amaya had left. It was my face he was looking into.

He gaped at me, his mouth opening and closing soundlessly, trying to make words, but only gasping air.

'Boo, motherfucker,' I whispered.

He jolted away in shock, falling off the couch in a befuddled heap.

I threw back my head and let out a long and cacophonous howl.

'Did the wittle boy have a wittle wee-wee accident?' I pointed to the pool of urine under him, spreading slowly, staining the spotless white carpet a pale yellow. But he didn't seem to notice, or care. He continued to stare at my face. He was now making shrill clucking sounds like a chicken.

I reached into my handbag and pulled out my machete.

'So much rust,' I complained, scratching at the dark curve of the blade and showing him the orange dust that settled on my fingertips.

'This belonged to a tender coconut seller I used to know. Sweet guy. He'd stand at the park where I used to do my runs. *Sathaku, sathaku, sathaku*, he'd slice at the coconuts, taking off the shell and the hard head first. *Sathaku, sathaku, sathaku*, he'd keep going until he got to the soft fleshy bits. I loved watching him.'

I leaned toward him and set the machete's blade at his neck. He recoiled from it, turning away.

'Smells awful, doesn't it? That's because I don't clean it.'

I pushed the blade into him, only hard enough to nick him: a few drops of blood trickled down to his shirt.

'Who are you? Where did Amaya go?' he whispered.

I ignored him. 'You're a good boy, aren't you? You'll do everything I tell you to do.'

His eyes went to the machete, then back again to my face. 'Good. Let's start with cash then. And some bling. Your stores have the most exquisite collection of diamonds and watches. I must say, your Appa has excellent taste.'

His face hardened. He looked again at the machete, but then shook his head this time. 'No,' he croaked. He swatted at the blade like it were a bothersome fly. 'No,' he said again, meeting my eyes defiantly.

I swung the blade at him. Without looking, without aiming. It made a long, deep gash across his chest.

'Not bad. A perfect arc,' I observed with satisfaction.

His eyes wide, he watched in mute horror as blood bloomed from the laceration, slowly, then gushed out, running down in torrents. He began to scream, but stopped when I put the blade to his mouth.

'Quiet down, or I will have to cut out your tongue,' I warned, and his cries fell into a whimper. 'You will obey me now, won't you?'

He nodded. He was blubbering like a child, snot and tears running down his face.

'What are you?' he asked again weakly, between sobs. And I howled again with laughter. 'Who are you? Where is Amaya? What happened to her face?'

'Amaya is resting,' I said, smiling sweetly. And I moved the machete back to his neck. 'She'll come out when I'm done with you.'

*** 

I didn't stop the car. I rolled down the window and leaned over to retch out an acrid spray of liquor and bile. The wind slapped back some of the vomit onto my face. I wiped myself clean on the sleeve of my shirt and kept driving. My body felt like it had managed to survive a train wreck, or a wild week-long orgy. My arms were sore from all the machete-swinging; when

I shifted gears, my shoulders creaked like old doors, sent jolts of sharp electric pain all the way down to my fingers. My head felt broken; it was spinning, making dizzying patterns out of the windscreen, night sky and asphalt.

'We're almost home,' Anani said chirpily. The tumour sat on my pelvic bone, now cold. Inside, her heart rested. Now calm.

I pressed harder on the accelerator. I had driven past only two cars so far, both drivers clearly intoxicated and zig-zagging down the empty road like they were still beating traffic. I reached into my handbag and pulled out a packet of cloves. I stuffed a few into my mouth and chewed them to a pulp, until my tongue got numb, lost all feeling. It would stop the nausea.

'Why don't you stop for a second, get off your ass and throw up. You're stinking up the car,' Anani grumbled.

'I don't want anyone seeing me.'

'There's no one here to see you, Amaya.'

'What about them?' I pointed to the dark shapes huddled on the pavement. Big like sacks, some of them turning and rolling about in their sleep. 'What if one of them wakes up, and sees my face well enough to go to the cops?'

'Stop being so paranoid!'

'Stop being a pain in my crotch, Anani,' I snarled back. 'It feels like I have a fireball stuck in my underwear sometimes.'

She laughed. It was an open, mirthful laughter. Like that of a child. I was tempted to laugh along, but held back.

'Oh, come on. Stop moping,' Anani said. 'We should be celebrating tonight. That motherfucker was loaded. He had a case of Rolexes just laying around his apartment, would you believe it?'

I smelled my fingers. Lemon-scented soap and Dettol. I kept sniffing, to see if I could detect anything else.

'I cleaned up well after us,' she said earnestly. 'I scrubbed the place down like I was his damn house-help. Got the door, the coffee table, the couch, the wine bottle and glasses, the drapes, everything we touched. No fingerprints, no hair, we've left nothing behind, Amaya.'

'But for a mutilated corpse,' I said wryly.

'Suddenly growing a conscience, are we?' Anani's voice was petulant. The tumour was becoming quickly warm, its flesh taut with tension.

'We've been doing this long enough, Amaya. Stop acting like Mother-fucking-Teresa.'

'I'm scared.' Tears filled my eyes. Bitter acid surged up my throat. There was nothing left in my stomach to throw up. I pressed a few more cloves into my mouth. 'This is the third one this month. The city's already on high alert.'

'I know. We're in the news,' she said proudly. 'They're calling it the Machete Murders.'

'They are hunting for us like rabid wolves.' I said, ignoring the delight in her voice. 'One little mistake, one careless piece of evidence, and it'll all be over, Anani.'

The tumour was clenched tight, hard as stone.

'Okay. We'll stop then. You can go back to working as a freelance designer and living in that dump with three other losers, scraping Maggi off disposable plates and sleeping on lumpy futons on the floor.'

'I just think we should slow down, Anani,' I said weakly. 'This is the third one this month,' I repeated.

'No, we'll stop. And you can kiss goodbye to that Paris trip you've been planning,' she said. 'Forget about the Louvre. Forget about sipping on champagne and gazing at Monet's *Water Lilies*.'

As I swerved into our apartment, my eyes went to the row of windows, counting up until I had reached Floor 11. I had left the drapes undrawn; I could see the flicker and dance of the television's lights inside our dark home. I couldn't wait to go in and draw us a warm bath, to soak in the suds, cleanse off the vomit, the blood, this night. Then I'd make us a tall glass of magic smoothie: a couple of Valium, a handful of painkillers, a few scoops of Milo and some honey, blended with milk and topped with marshmallows. We would curl up with it in front of the TV, let the sounds lull us to sleep.

'Musée de l'Orangerie. That's where the *Water Lilies* are displayed,' I said, switching off the ignition and rolling up the windows. Anani was right. The car did stink. I would have to get it cleaned. 'Not the Louvre.'

I leaned back in my seat and closed my eyes. I touched the tumour fondly, gently. 'I want to take you there, Anani. I want to take you everywhere. See the world with you,' I whispered. I patted at her, humming softly, soothing her. I caressed the skin over my pelvic bone until it cooled. I could feel her heart steadying under my touch, the lump softening, becoming slack. She was asleep within moments. It had been a long night. She needed the rest. Soon, it would be time again. For Anani to awaken.

\*\*\*

'You said you liked getting inked.' His eyes searched her body, roving. 'But I don't see any tattoos on you.'

'They aren't on display,' Amaya said, flipping her hair, flashing him a coquettish smile. Then she lifted the hem of her skirt: on one ankle was a dark cloud with raindrops spilling out, and on the other was a large calligraphic 'A'.

'A for Amaya. That's your name,' he guessed drunkenly. Stupidly.

'No. A for Anani,' Amaya corrected. 'Anani means 'cloud'.'

'The motherfucker doesn't need to know all this. Stick to the script,' I snapped.

'Who's Anani?' he asked.

Amaya did not answer him. She peeled her top's strap off her right shoulder, revealing a miniature of *The Starry Night* above her breast, the blues deep, the yellows bright, the colours swirling and rolling like real paint. One of Amaya's favourites. She wanted to have it painted on our ceiling too, so she could fall asleep staring at it.

'This is a famous painting by Van Gogh… You must've seen this before,' she said.

He shook his head. 'Van who?'

'Oh, you uncultured prick. Even a child knows this one,' I growled.

He reached to touch the tattoo eagerly, but she had already fixed her top and moved away from him, nimble as a cat. Amaya scooped up her hair and turned to one side: on the back of her neck was a circle, pitch-black, and inside it, two roses, the colour of fresh-drawn blood.

'This is beautiful,' he said. 'What does it mean?' He had his fingers on her neck within moments, stroking, rubbing.

'Like you really care. Take your hands off her, you fat fuck,' I screamed. I could feel my pulse quicken with anger.

'It's a womb,' Amaya explained, unruffled by his touch. 'And the two roses floating inside its dark waters are my twin sister and I.'

'Twins? That must be nice. Two for the price of one, they say,' he said smirking. 'Are you guys identical?'

'Fraternal.'

'Sounds kind of hot. I'd like to see you both together.'

'You cannot.'

'And why not?'

'Because I ate her,' Amaya said.

He laughed, shaking his head, snorting, as if she had cracked a joke.

'I swallowed her whole.' my sister went on, speaking in hushed, dramatic whispers.

'Stop it, Amaya. Stop oversharing, you dumbass,' I warned. She was clearly inebriated. She tended to do this sometimes. Amaya loved telling them our story.

Why must they know, I would ask.

How does it matter if they know? she would say. They won't tell. They'll take our secret to the grave, won't they?

I really couldn't argue with this.

'Beating heart, twitching limbs, thrumming brain, breathing lungs, I ate all of it. I ate all of her. In the womb. One morning, my mother went in for her ultrasound and discovered that my twin had vanished. Gone. Just like that,' she said, snapping her fingers, smiling woefully. 'There was just me. Guess I had gotten a little too hungry inside.'

He was quiet. Uncomfortable – they all were when they heard our story.

'That sucks,' he finally said.

'No shit, Einstein. It does suck.'

My sister sniffled all of a sudden, then slumped her shoulders. She wiped at her eyes. I couldn't help but laugh. The little weasel was playing him like a fucking fiddle.

'No one cared that she was gone. My father wanted sons. He didn't want girls – not one, certainly not two. He might have liked it better if I were gone too.' Amaya drew in a sharp breath, like she was about to burst into tears.

'Nice move,' I chuckled. 'Reel him in nice and slow, Amaya. All these dicks have a saviour complex.'

'Hey, don't say that. Don't cry,' he cooed, and wrapped an arm around her, trying to comfort her. Amaya drew him into a tight embrace. She laid her head on his chest, pressed her mouth to his neck. He moaned. He was clearly getting aroused.

'There's another tattoo,' she said softly. 'A special one. I don't show it to everyone,' she said softly.

'Can I see it?' he asked.

Amaya smiled. She pulled down the elastic waistline of her skirt and bent over so he could see. On our lower back, it would be: a bird with a gigantic body and two heads, the faces like that of hawks, eyes watchful and feral and filled with shades of fire, plumage blazing golden, talons long and curved like blades, dripping scarlet blood. A bird of prey. Swooping, wings spread, on the brink of attack.

'Gandaberunda,' she said.

# RULEBOOK FOR CREATING A UNIVERSE

## TASHAN MEHTA

In an island that floats at the beginning of time, there is a *Rulebook for Creating a Universe*. This book is old, with instructions on how to make forever worlds. It says, 'When stitching a universe, think carefully about the kind of sun you want. Will it be hot or cold, moss or vein? Your sun will last forever and your planetary colour palettes will depend on it. Choose wisely. Follow the blueprint.'

Beloved, you know this story.

You know Yukti is a weaver on this island-before-time and that she hates weaving. Her mother must put the lotus stalk in her hand and even then she will scowl at the water until her mother says, *Faster Mu-mu, we don't own time!* So Yukti – who also hates the nickname Mu-mu – will snap open the stalk to reveal filaments of silver that she thinks look like spit. These are the fibres of Time. She will rub them together to make a thread and begin stitching the banana leaf she is assigned.

This is how a single universe is made – on this island, one leaf at a time. Leaves make a tree. Trees and rivers make a planet, planets create a galaxy, and galaxies form a universe. Small to large. This is what Yukti's mother tells her as she brushes her daughter's hair at night. She wants Yukti to apply herself. *We're doing good work, Mu-mu.* Her daughter leans back into her chest, happy. *Are you listening to me?* Her daughter shakes her head, giggling. *You're not listening to me, you shaitan.* Her mother tickles her until Yukti squeals.

On days her mother takes pity on her, Yukti is sent to harvest the lotuses. This she loves. She's the only girl on the boat but she belongs – even the men know it. They send her into the thick patches of lotuses, where the boat cannot push its nose, and she wades among petals as large as her torso. The water, which is biting cold, grows warmer when she clutches a lotus stem, then hot when she holds the slippery knife and hacks through it.

Her brother tells her, in conspiratorial whispers, that this is because the lotuses go all the way down to the beginning of time.

But there is nothing in her life until now, nothing really, that explains why the lotuses one day bend their heads and begin talking to her.

\*\*\*

Yukti doesn't understand the lotuses' language. It is colour that blooms across her mind, the scent of faint perfume, trails of thought that writhe and curl like reeds. It changes her. One day she blinks and the island dissipates, breaking into a zillion fine particles of gold dust. She blinks again and the world coalesces, regrowing its outlines. She trembles.

She begins to dream of volcanoes.

She doesn't know what a volcano is. They've never made one on this island. She tries to describe it to her brother and he tells her that she means a melted sun, that's all. So she starts thinking of suns.

*Apoi, why can't we make suns?*

Her best friend Apoi puts down the fern she is stitching and thinks. They are sitting on a platform that floats on the endless water of their island. Water and lotuses, that's all their island-before-time is made of. Apoi thinks hard. It is not a normal question; no one here asks these things. But Apoi is the best student in the village and so she finds an answer.

*Because suns are big and require strength*, she explains. *Boys are stronger. Girls have deft fingers and so can stitch forests and rivers.*

Yukti wasn't looking for the textbook version. *We can do it too*, she says, surly but under her breath. Apoi doesn't hear.

The *Rulebook for Creating a Universe* talks about the lotuses. It says, 'Beware. Lotuses may shimmer and turn to gold dust when you hold them. Ignore this. Hold fast and cut the stalk as low as you can reach. If the lotuses talk, don't listen. Never listen.'

Yukti has listened.

*Ma?*

*Yes, Mu-mu?*

*Why don't you make suns?*

Her mother stops stirring her lotus stew. She is more perceptive than Apoi, so she says, *Why do you ask?*

But Yukti knows this sidestepping tactic. *Have you tried?* she asks. She doesn't know that her voice is growing shriller, as it does when she is upset.

*No*, her mother says gently. *But —*

*Why not?* Aggressive now.

*Because I don't want to.* Her mother continues stirring her stew, deciding that the best way to deal with this tantrum is to ignore it.

*I don't believe you.*

*Yukti —* Stern now.

*I don't believe you. And if you had tried, only tried, then maybe I could stitch them too!*

Yukti is sent to bed without supper. She lies on her mat and feels her skin boil, itching to erupt. She is filled with a bottomless want; she wants to know who decided the things she could and could not do; she wants to scream. The lotus voices whisper.

Later, when her mother kneels by her mat and asks if she wants her hair brushed, Yukti says no with venom. Then she cries into her mother's lap, with large heaving sobs, as her mother strokes her hair soothingly.

\*\*\*

They stop Yukti from going out with the boats.

Her mother tries to hide her madness from the village but they learn of it. Yukti is now seeing three of everything. She is saying nonsense words in her sleep. The elders meet and remember the teachings of their ancestors. They have an important task here on this island — they are responsible for all creation. Each task in their society has been carefully crafted to fulfil this purpose of building universes; each person must play their role. A girl must never go to the lotus fields — it only spreads disaster.

The elders visit Yukti's family. They tell her father to mind his daughter; they comfort Yukti's mother, who trembles at what Yukti may become.

That night, after the elders leave, her mother makes lotus tea. She sits alone in the dark, steeping over the problem.

She knows her baby better than anyone else. The elders think the problem is small, some vague babbling, but she knows how far it has gone. Her daughter's eyes are seeing further than they are meant to see. Her grandmother got like that once. They blinded her in fear.

She cannot let that happen to her baby.

From then on, she watches Yukti like a hawk. She makes her weave on a cushion opposite her, in her shadow; if Yukti goes to play, she follows. Her brother is forbidden to tell his sister folktales; her husband is made to wash all trace of lotuses off him before entering the house.

Yukti doesn't complain.

Instead, she weaves better. She stops talking in her sleep and smiles when she's supposed to, even though the smile doesn't reach her eyes. Once, her mother catches her drawing a mountain with a hollow inside, but when she blinks Yukti has rubbed the drawing away – and she doesn't know if she imagined it.

She must have.

Yukti becomes the best weaver in the village. She is praised; neighbours drop in at the house to admire her work and stay till they are offered free tea. Yukti's mother pretends to be proud. She thinks of the hollow mountain and wishes her daughter's smile would reach her eyes.

Then, one day, Yukti glances up from the glow lamp as she kneels beside her mat and looks – really looks – at her mother.

Yukti's eyes are wide, as large as the day her mother gave birth to her. Then she says *Ma* and holds out her arms.

Her mother collapses into them. She holds her daughter close, pressing her nose into her daughter's neck, breathing in. When Yukti pulls away and smiles, it reaches her eyes.

That night Yukti's mother brushes her hair slowly and languidly. They drink lotus tea. They laugh, warm in their love for each other. Then, when the sky is covered with gold-black, Yukti slips out of her mat, past her sleeping family who dream dreams of content, down the stairs and into the cold, where she unties the boat from its moorings and slips it, eel-like, into the catfish-black water.

You know where she is going.

\*\*\*

The *Rulebook for Creating a Universe* talks a lot about the lotuses. It has 547 rules on the flowers, all of them warnings. Rule 89 is in bold. It says, 'You are not a hero. Lotuses seduce. You are not immune to that seduction. Stay humble and work with the group. Stitch with direction, with the softness of certainty. Never stray.'

The water is emptier than Yukti remembers. Across each mile of glass, she sees the ghosts of lotuses now cut; their dead forms leave gold dust in the air. Yukti knows she is the only one who can see this, just like she is the only one who notices that the stalks the boats bring are yellow. The lotuses are dying. The village is farming too far and too fast; Time is running out.

She wishes her mother could see.

When the lotuses appear, they do so suddenly; Yukti is dwarfed by their petals, each flower eager to touch her skin.

They are happy; they have been waiting for her. Her boat is nosed forward with trembling lotus pads; petal tips play with her hair. She laughs. She feels alive, understood. All her fear disappears.

The boat comes to a halt. Yukti waits. Nothing happens. The lotuses watch her. She watches them. Gold dust floats as if on the breath of an invisible creature.

Yukti grows sleepy and leans against the side of the boat. Gently, almost listlessly, she dips her fingers in –

– The water erupts. Gold fans out in all directions; something wraps around her wrist and yanks her in. She thrashes, panicked, but more stems curl around her legs and arms. She fights. She opens her mouth to say please, but water pours down her gullet; the lake closes over her head with a woooosh. The last thing she sees is the lotuses, hazy through the water. They look hungry.

*\*\**

In the beginning, there were ideas. They streamed through the void as gold particles, content to go nowhere. Then similar ideas began to coalesce. They moved out of the neat lines they followed and clustered into logical order – this idea first, that particle second, and so on. In this way, they made Time.

These threads spun themselves into an island, floating in the void. They curled into seeds and became lotuses so that they could open their faces to the void, feel its cool touch. They wanted to have faces. They called to their brothers and sisters still journeying across the void; they asked them to join the island and feel what it was to be. Several did. They rained down and melted and bumped into the lake you now drown in.

They even made you, bronze-skinned and yellow-eyed. They gave you only one command: make. But you listened wrong.

*Why are you telling me this?* Yukti asks.

She is floating in water that is golden, green and blue in different shimmers, like it cannot make up its mind. She isn't breathing, so she must be dead. But the heart of the island is staring at her like she is anything but.

Why did you come to us? the heart asks.

Yukti doesn't know how to translate her yearning into the lotuses' language. She wants to burst out of her skin and flower into a jungle so complex no one could weave it. So instead she says, *You are dying.*

You heard wrong, the heart says. When did we ask you to snap us open and weave with our innards? What use is dead Time to you, silver like old hair? You were meant to shape the void as we shaped you – by tilting your head to the sky and listening to where the ideas wanted to go. When did you grow deaf?

\*\*\*

Yukti wakes because she has to vomit. She vomits and vomits, emptying all the water in her. Then she curls up on the boat's smooth belly and waits for morning. When it comes, she holds the paddle in her shivering hand and rows home. It takes her longer because she's tired and the paddle keeps slipping from her grip. When she pulls into the village, it is almost afternoon.

Her community watches her. They discovered Yukti was missing in the middle of the night; her brother raised the alarm. When her mother found the boat gone, her heart sank. But by then it was too late.

The village's activities lie abandoned; the villagers stand, grave, at the edges of their stilted houses. Yukti can see Apoi, her eyes like petrified pebbles, her mouth forming a similar 'O'. Yukti doesn't stop; she rows until she reaches her house. When she climbs the stairs slowly, she finds her mother waiting for her. When she dips through the doorway, her mother backs up against the wall, frightened.

In the house's cool interior, Yukti realizes why. She is glowing.

*Mu-mu?*

Yukti nods.

*Where were you, Mu-mu?* Her mother takes a step forward. This girl is her baby, her beloved baby who kept trying to eat her thumb when she born and who laughs like a drunken man, in great big hiccupping hiccups. She will not be scared of her.

Yukti tells her. She knows she must go to the elders with this story but she wants to tell her mother. Besides, she is only fourteen and her parents are still an authority of a sort, even though it is not spelt with a capital A.

So she describes how universes are being built with dead Time, spinning suns that cannot die and so do not truly live. Nothing will change in those galaxies; trees will not grow or shed leaves; rivers will not swell or fade. Mountains will always know only one height – the height the villagers gave them. In time, the dye will fade to reveal the silver weave from which the worlds were made; then this too will grow pale, caking into white ash. Creation will spin with burnt remains, until these too will flake and be swallowed by the void.

Her mother closes her eyes. Her child is mad.

So Yukti shows her. She unfurls the hand she's kept clutched this whole time to reveal a lotus bud, its petals parted in a surprised and embarrassed breath, its roots intact. She lifts it to her lips and blows. Gold dust settles into her mother's eyes.

\*\*\*

Beloved, you have been in this story. Versions of it play across time, on loop. It's in your bones.

So, remember. Breathe through your fear and pull up the strands of this story. The elders will not listen. There's Yukti, clutching onto her mother as they pull her away. She's frightened, confused. She's telling them what they cannot see; she's only trying to save them. Why won't they listen?

She finds no answer. Her mother is hysterical. She's fighting with the villagers, trying to get to her child. She's saying, *It's only make-believe, she doesn't mean it, she takes it back, she takes it back.* Yukti's father is shouting. Yukti's brother tries to reach his parents and finds the crowd shrinks away from him, like he is diseased.

Yukti looks for Apoi in the pandemonium, the smartest person in the village, the best student. *You have to listen to them*, she shouts, hoping her best friend can hear her. She will understand. *You have to let it become.*

Apoi looks away.

After that, Yukti stops fighting. They drag her out.

Yukti is branded hysterical. Her mother is blamed for this new epidemic of lotus madness. Her father is disciplined, her brother ostracized. If you look closely, you can see her mother's eyes grow hard in a way that scares Yukti's father. You can hear the echoes of Yukti's last words as they tie her to a boat, rippling in the still air. *Listen — why won't you listen?*

Fear hardens.

The community pulls together. Scribes draft the *Rulebook for Creating a Universe*. Artists sketch the first official blueprint. Copies are made. Keepers are appointed. The *Rulebook* is taught in special schools. Children quiz children on its details, a game. Girls who stitch leaves make sure they copy the veins exactly. Precision is praised.

And Yukti, the girl who won't stop glowing, is locked in a house built specially for her, far away from the village. She is left to starve. But she doesn't starve. She eats the gold dust she can scoop from the water by thrusting her hands into the gap in the floor. She listens to her heart shrink until she believes it cannot get any smaller. She stares out of the window as the lotus fields dwindle. They're crying out for her help. She has nothing left to give.

All this is the story.

Now remember the parts they don't tell you.

Like how everything is built like a volcano — planets, universes, bodies — with molten change sitting in our bellies. How the lock on Yukti's jail clicks one night and the door pops open. How five women stand in the doorway, carved by the amber moon. A silhouette of a lotus flower, now fully grown and its roots trailing the floor, hangs from one of their hands.

*Some things*, Yukti's mother says as she presses her daughter to her chest and they cry with an emotion that cannot be held in language, *can only be done in silence, at night.*

\*\*\*

Six women stand waist deep in empty water. Gold whirls around them. Yukti turns to her mother, her glow faint now, and says in a small voice, *I don't know what to do.*

But her mother is having none of it. She runs her fingers through Yukti's hair, feeling the strands knot between her knuckles. Her baby. *You only have to listen*, she says. Her voice is so sure and full of love. It steadies Yukti.

Yukti takes a deep breath and closes her eyes.

They build a universe out of gold dust, collecting in their palms from the water. The particles flock to them, eager. The women shape with their fingers, asking the particles which ones they would like to join with.

Yukti's yearning fills her. It mixes with her fear and her hope. Who knows what tomorrow will bring? She may never see another light or get this chance again. So she crumbles her fear and gives in to her yearning, letting it rise in her like a molten wave. She pours it into the universe she's shaping. When the particles in her hand begin to vibrate, she knows they will never be content to stay in a single sequence.

The women weave small and fine and tight, so that when they are done, the whole universe sits on Yukti's palm, no bigger than a gold speck. Clutching it very gently in her nails, Yukti pulls her arm back as far as it will go. She flings the speck into the void, where it disappears.

The *Rulebook for Creating a Universe* mentions Yukti only once. It does not take her name. It says, 'Remember the girl who tried to steal Time to weave a universe. Remember that in her universe suns die and they call god a woman. Do not let that be your daughter.'

***

Yukti's seed, pushed deep into the void's skin, will burst. It will carry colours of its own. The particles in it will link and dissolve and link again into formations that will burn our eyes when viewed through our telescopes. It will create mountains that crush us and ocean depths we cannot touch. It will spiral up and down and up, the dunes of existence. We will keep trying to cross them.

It will have volcanoes.

But let us leave grandeur to science. Let us leave language to itself. Get up and go into the sun, beloved, to the edge of a world that houses you. You are on a beach. You've spent the morning scared of a future you cannot predict. You've spent the afternoon trying to map out different possibilities to create a rulebook of your own. You've prayed to this universe for the only thing it cannot give you: Certainty.

Now let it go. Breathe in the salt. Watch the gold glint on the crest of a wave.

Then walk to where the crabs make their maps and the sea tries to drown them. Let a wave recede and press your toe into the wet sand it leaves behind. Watch it erupt into gold.

This is your inheritance. Listen.

# THE DEMON HUNTER'S DILEMMA

## SAMHITA ARNI

Magic still exists, in patches and tiny pockets in this world. One such pocket lies at the heart of the Hasdeo Arand forest, screened from the cities and eyes of men by its dense, verdant cover. Here, creatures — the sort that you hear about in the tales and myths of your childhood, like the vidhyadharas wheeling through the air and the makaras who bathe in forest rivers — thrive. That's why Antara was here. A pisacha had been spotted near the village of Kendai, and her guru had dispatched her to deal with the threat and bring back the monster to his ashram, deep in the Aravallis.

This was the first mission he had entrusted to Antara alone. And since he was everything to her — mother, father, teacher — she was determined to do it right. It was also the first time that she was on her own, away from her guru and his hilltop ashram shielded by force fields of magic created by mantras long forgotten, mantras that only her guru had knowledge of.

Antara knew little of the outside world, the world that had birthed her. Her guru had taken her in as an infant, abandoned in a city in this world – and raised her to be his own. She remembered being taken along on one of his trips, as a young child, to a city where concrete towers thrust into the sky and machine-birds whirled in the air. She had clung tightly to his hand, and asked to go back to the ashram. This was the world that had rejected her, she had told him, and she wanted no part of it. He had smiled his usual inscrutable smile. When they returned, her training had begun in earnest.

The rustle of leaves brought her back to the present. Antara held her breath. The pisacha had been coming to this very spot, every night, for the past two weeks. He was silent, so silent you could miss him, and when he moved it was with graceful, quiet economy. But Antara knew exactly where he was, his shape outlined by moonlight. She had been observing him from closer quarters each night, a black form hovering at the edge of the horizon, blotting out a patch of stars.

She knew she had to be careful, for pisachas had quick reflexes. In absolutely no time he could transform into the flesh-eating demon rendered in detail in the palm-leaf manuscripts that lined her guru's library, a creature that would plague human society; eating men, women and even children.

Antara drew in a deep breath and tried to focus. She would have to shoot the arrow and recite the mantra her guru had instructed her in. It was in a strange, alien tongue she had never quite mastered; it had taken her months to perfect her pronunciations. It was a mantra that would cause the arrow to transform into a diamond snare, a web of light that would split into strings of diamonds binding and capturing any creature in a prison impossible to escape.

She had done this before, ensnaring vidhyadharas whom she would take back to her guru's hermitage in the heart of the forest, where he would then drain them of their life force, their shakti.

'This is what happens to those who are dangerous,' he had said when, as a little girl, she had strayed into his laboratory with a million questions on her mind. It was a strange place filled with bizarre equipment and lined with bottles and jars of all sizes. 'Those who are evil, we take their power from them and use it for good,' he had said, something inexplicable gleaming in his eyes. He had forbidden her to enter the laboratory ever again without his permission and so she never did. And he had never mentioned it since either. It was like the laboratory didn't exist within the walls of the ashram. Antara never found out what went on in there, just as she never mustered up the courage to ask her guru how exactly he used the life force of the captured creatures for 'good'. She just did as he commanded because he was her mentor. No questions asked. She had trained her mind to put her curiosity at rest so it would be free to learn and master the mantras she needed for her missions.

This was her first time hunting pisachas. Now the pisacha was right at the tree that she had climbed on to secure a good vantage point, so close she could hear him breathing. He was larger than she had expected, dwarfing her. She fretted. Would she be able to take him down and secure him?

The pisacha moved, and the moonlight glinted off his black, smooth back. His muscles rippled, sinuous, and then he turned his face towards her.

Antara had never been this close to any of the creatures she hunted. Her skills in archery ensured she could hit her target from over a hundred paces away. But now, at such proximity, she was taken aback.

In her mind, pisachas were flesh-eating monsters, with the sharp fangs, red lolling tongues and decomposing, rotting bodies illustrated in the scrolls and manuscripts tucked away in her guru's library. But the creature before her was nothing like the illustrations that she had pored over for hours. His skin was smooth, and though his fangs were sharp and glistening, they were by no means repulsive. His eyes glimmered with an unusual light, his body was sculpted, ridges of muscle along his ribs. A silver amulet glimmered on a toned chest. Moonlight fell across the hard, angular planes of his face. He was…beautiful.

She sucked in her breath.

The pisacha whipped around, startled by the sound.

'Oh,' he exclaimed, catching sight of her, 'a pretty girl.'

Antara was taken aback. She almost slipped from the branch she was balanced on, and put a hand out to steady herself.

The pisacha's eyes sparkled. 'What are you doing here all alone?'

The sound of his voice astonished Antara. It was seductive, and something in it whispered of caresses and kisses. Of dark pleasures, silken sheets and bodies slick with sweat. Antara shook her head as though to clear it. No, she would not give in to his sorcery. Focusing with all her might, she let her arrow fly. As she recited the mantra, honed by years of practice, the arrow burst into a thousand shimmering strings that fastened into a cage around the pisacha.

He shrieked as the strings cut into his skin, binding him tightly.

'What have you done to me?' He screamed again, and twisted, falling to the ground beneath them, branches splintering as he fell past them.

Antara leapt quickly from branch to branch until she hit the ground, and trained her bow on him.

The pisacha, trapped in the diamond snare, glared at her, grimacing in discomfort, blood trickling from wounds where bits of bark had got embedded in his skin during the fall. 'Why are you doing this?' he growled.

'You are a pisacha,' Antara replied. 'You're evil. You kill people.'

He shook his head. 'No, you've got it all wrong!'

'No, I haven't!' she shouted, determined to shut him up. The creatures she had captured before had tried to impress her with their strength, or begged for mercy. This one did neither. For some reason, that made her blood boil. 'My guru...'

The pisacha interrupted her. 'Who is your guru?' he asked through gritted teeth.

'The one who hunted the vetalas to extinction a thousand years ago,' Antara said with a sneer.

The pisacha's eyes widened. 'Him! You think *I'm* bad, that *I* feast on the flesh of your unborn children? Is your teacher any different? Him, with his fancy ashram and that sinister laboratory... I know about that place.'

'You're evil,' Antara spat out.

The pisacha shook his head. 'Not all of us. Some of you humans, too, you imprison us in these cages. What does that make you?'

Antara's temper flared. 'I'm not – ' She stopped herself. What was the point? The pisacha was her prisoner. She took a deep breath, 'I don't have to listen to you...' A faint image of the containers in her guru's laboratory returned to her mind. She brushed it away instantly.

She whistled, and her chariot materialized. It was nothing like the chariots of old. It was one her guru had designed, using the technologies of the time and the mantras of yore to fashion a horse-less chariot that could travel through the three worlds. At any other time, she would have spent an entire day replenishing her *tapas*, her power, and then recite the mantras that would enable the chariot to zoom through space and time and emerge on the other side of the country, in the Aravallis. But now, impatient to be on her way, she hoisted the cage onto the floor of the chariot by means of another mantra and, taking her place on the driver's seat, guided the vehicle deeper into the forest.

'Listen! You must free me,' the pisacha whispered, his voice low and urgent.

She shook her head. 'No.'

'There are tales about your guru – you may not have heard them,' he persisted. 'How he dissects creatures like me and inspects us in that secret laboratory of his. Performs experiments on us to drain us of our powers and then offers them to men of this world, for a fortune.'

Antara could feel his gaze on her, but kept her silence. She remembered the visitors in her guru's ashram. Famous, rich people. Actors. Politicians. Celebrities. Military leaders. People who lusted for power, for fame. His own rise to renown and subsequent power had always been a mystery to her… No, her guru…it couldn't possibly be true. 'No!'

'Come on, you must have seen something,' said the pisacha.

Yes, she had. Another memory slowly swirled into her head. She had once watched, hidden, as her guru had dragged in a many-armed asura bound by diamantine ropes. The asura had screeched in pain as her guru cut off his arms, one by one, and placed them in jars. Yet again she firmly swatted the memory away.

'Shut up,' she snapped. Then she picked up a stone and tossed it behind her.

'Ouch.' The pisacha groaned as the stone hit its target.

Antara smirked.

As the sun rose, she drove the chariot into a cave, for sunlight would harm the pisacha. Slanting rays of light illuminated the walls of the cavern. She needed to rest so that she could channel the power to recite the mantras for her onward journey, which meant they would have to stay here for a day at least. As she tethered her horse, she noticed, much to her surprise, that a faint sheen of sweat glittered on the pisacha's skin. His brow was contorted, as if he was in pain. Was he ill?

His eyes widened as she approached him to take a closer look. For some reason that Antara could not put her finger on, this made her feel self-conscious.

'How old are you?' he asked suddenly.

'Nineteen,' she found herself replying.

'So young, so beautiful, and so full of hate.' He closed his eyes.

Antara was surprised. Beautiful? This blood-thirsty pisacha thought she was beautiful? She turned away quickly, confused, and began pacing up and down the cave.

He groaned.

Antara kept her face turned away. No, she wasn't going to engage with him. But she peered at him from the corner of her eyes. Oh no, she sighed inwardly. His skin had lost its sheen, and he had turned lifeless and dull. She rushed over to him. It was obvious that something was wrong. His eyes had glazed over and he seemed to be in the grip of some strange delirium.

'Skies,' he shouted out. 'Blue skies!'

Taken aback, Antara watched him cautiously for a while. Then she retracted the diamond snare and walked around him, stopping when she noticed a gash on his leg. It must be from tha fall, she figured, and the gash was now oozing blood and pus. He was in no condition to travel. They would have to remain in the cave while he recovered, causing a further delay in their journey.

Her guru would not be pleased.

Minutes crept by, and the pisacha moaned again in his sleep. Antara bit her nails. What could she do? She needed to get him to the ashram as soon as she could. As she cast about in her mind for a solution, she remembered the plant that grew in the hills not far from the cave, perhaps a couple of hours' journey on foot; she would leave the chariot here. She could crush the leaves to make a balm to heal any wound – just like her guru had taught her.

She set protective spells around the cave and, instead of binding the creature with the diamond snare, fastened it across the mouth of the cave, creating a prison he would not be able to leave.

Then she set off for the hills.

It took her the rest of the day, and part of the night, to return with the herb. As she collected the water from a nearby pond to turn the powdered herb into a paste, she stopped, catching sight of her reflection in the dark water.

Long hair, eyes that seemed too big for her face. Lips that she had always thought too plump. A nose that she had wished was less sharp. Yet, the pisacha had called her beautiful.

She frowned. Really?

She had never considered herself beautiful. Not even pretty. No one had ever told her she was pretty before. She shook her head. Such thoughts had no place in her mind. She needed to focus on the task at hand – to ensure the pisacha regained his strength and take him back to her guru.

She applied the paste to his wounds and waited anxiously. She sat sleepless the entire night – watching him, for a sign, for anything that would indicate he was recovering. It was when the skies mildly lightened that she dozed off, only to awaken with a start when she felt a caress on her arm.

It was the pisacha. He was awake. Antara leapt to her feet. Moving quickly to her prisoner, she examined him. He was still weak but his breathing was even and his skin was regaining its former colour. The herb had worked.

'Thank you,' he said, then paused, scrutinizing her face. 'Tell me again…why do you hate us?' he asked.

'You kill humans.' She fell silent, not intending to say more, but under his insistent gaze the words tumbled out. 'You are my enemy.'

The pisacha stared at her. 'How sad,' he whispered, 'that you believe that.'

A hundred thoughts rushed through her head. 'I –' she stuttered and then stopped. What could she say?

'You know, I was not born like this.'

Antara looked up at him.

He continued. 'Not all of us are. Some of us are cursed into becoming a pisacha. I was a kinnara once. I had beautiful wings and eyes like a hawk. How I miss my wings, and flying in the sunlight.'

His eyes turned wistful. 'I dream of it, still.' He turned away.

Something in Antara stirred as she watched him. The gentle rise and fall of his chest, the strange, faraway look in his eyes. No, she tried to tell herself. He was the enemy...

In spite of herself, she asked, 'What will reverse your curse?'

He laughed; a bitter, hollow laugh. 'True love, I believe.'

'True love? Do you believe in that?'

'Don't you?' He gazed at her intently.

Antara felt like a deer pinioned by a hunter's arrow. She shook her head.

The pisacha waited for an instant before replying. 'I think I must,' he said. 'It's all that's left for me.'

'What is the kingdom of the kinnaras like?' Antara found herself asking. This conversation was one she should be walking away from she told herself, but she wasn't able to. Somehow, she was here. She wanted to know more.

His face lit up at the question, and he told her about his homeland. How, in the skies, past the clouds, there existed the nomadic kingdom of the kinnaras, winged creatures with bodies of men. There, nests were built on vast clouds, forming homes that itinerantly travelled the skies, borne by the wind. How there were different tribes among the kinnaras, with differently patterned and coloured wings: there was the tribe that lived in the north, on the clouds over the North Pole, with wings the colour of azure seas, and a tribe that lived in homes that hovered over the tropics, their wings sporting feathers in scarlet and crimson.

On one night each year, he told her, the tribes would congregate to dance till the sun rose the next dawn. There was nothing as dazzling as the sight of hundreds of kinnaras, pirouetting into the sky, wings spread out – a stunning riot of colours.

'There's nothing as beautiful...' He paused to look at her. 'What about your home?' he asked.

'Nothing like yours,' she replied flatly. 'It's an ashram. Discipline, obedience, lessons – that's what it is about. From morning to evening.'

'Why do you stay there?'

Antara shrugged. 'Because my guru raised me, gave me a roof, training – taught me everything I know. I owe him my loyalty.'

The pisacha did not reply. Instead, he turned away from her and lay down. Almost immediately, his breaths grew deeper and Antara realized he was asleep. She knew she should sleep too, rest before the journey that night to her guru's ashram. But she could not. Abruptly, she began to wonder what a life outside the ashram, beyond the stern eyes of her guru, would be like.

What flying like a kinnara would be like.

She dreamt of sun-kissed clouds, and flapping wings, and the thrill of feeling the wind in her face. At some point, her imaginings turned into fantasy. She felt the pisacha's hands on her, blazing a trail of fire down her body. His skin felt warm to the touch, and it tasted of salt. She felt his lips on her before they drifted down, venturing over the length of her body. The pleasure she felt was unbearable, as if she were about to explode...

Antara awoke with a jerk out of her reverie.

Night had fallen. The pisacha was awake, staring at her, a strange smile on his lips.

Did he know what she had been thinking about? Antara felt her face burn.

'It's time we left,' she said brusquely and began to recite the mantra that would transport her and the pisacha to her guru's ashram.

They arrived just as a trace of pink begun to creep around the edges of the sky, and the sun began to rise on the ashram. Its spires thrust upwards, ringed by walls made of stone that provided the perfect defence. The shimmer in the air above the structure spoke of the magic that protected her home. She frowned. She had never thought of it before — but it looked more like a fortress than a hermitage. Why did her guru have so many enemies? Why was no one allowed in that laboratory of his? What did he do with the life force he extracted from the monsters? Why did this place need so many magical enforcements to keep others out?

She brushed the thoughts aside, and saying, 'Here we are,' turned to the pisacha.

His face was like stone, frozen with fear. She felt something stirring in her heart. No, a voice — her guru's — screamed in her mind. He is evil! He is a demon. He is the enemy! But still her heart continued to twist. She could no longer avoid the memories she had blocked out for so long. They came back now, violent and bloody as they were. Her guru standing red-eyed beside the decapitated asura, licking the blood that dripped from the severed head. He had seemed to grow stronger with each lick, as though a new life force had been added to his own... Somewhere in the recesses of her soul Antara knew the truth now, and it changed everything.

'I...I can't do it!' Antara shouted. 'I will not!' Turning to the pisacha, she retracted the diamond snare.

The pisacha peered at her. 'What – '

Antara exhaled deeply. 'I can't do this to you.'

He stood before her, dumbfounded, unmoving.

'Go, you're free!' she said urgently.

Antara saw his eyes soften, his mouth stretch into a smile, and to her his smile felt like the rising sun. In that moment he reached out for her – and she for him. Their palms touched. She lifted her face to his. Their lips met. The warmth of a thousand fires exploded beneath her skin. Fire seethed under her fingertips. Something rustled in the forest behind them – Antara opened her eyes.

And there, in a trice, the pisacha had changed. Fire lit his eyes, and large golden-brown wings fanned out from either side.

'Oh!' Antara exclaimed.

'The spell,' he said, 'you broke it...'

He held out his hand. 'Come –'

Antara stared at him. If she took his hand it would mean leaving behind her guru, the ashram, the life she knew.

She reached forward, and then stopped. No, she couldn't. Her guru had cared for her. She owed him her loyalty. Loyalty to what, a voice in her mind piped up. To killing beautiful, magical creatures for selfish profit? What she had been brought up to believe, she suddenly realized as she gazed at the pisacha's golden-brown wings, was entirely false. And, young as she was, Antara had believed her guru blindly. Always. Until now. She realized that many of the creatures her guru had killed were neither dangerous, nor evil. They were beautiful. It was her guru who had failed to see their beauty, their aliveness. He had tried to stamp out everything that was different and unique ends and instead used their magic for his own ends.

The world changed for Antara in that instant.

She looked at the spellbinding form in front of her, and he nodded gently, for now he could see the truth in her eyes.

'Come,' he whispered, still holding out his hand. 'Come with me.' Antara reached out, and together they soared towards the clouds.

# EARTH AND EVOLUTION WALK INTO A BAR...

## SEJAL MEHTA

The olive green van prowling the tiny lanes of the city was fairly inconspicuous, with just two doors in the front, a solid body and a double door at the back. It was the kind of vehicle you would use to ferry cargo. A heavy winter mist, so rare in this coastal city, settled snugly around everything as the van cruised past evening markets and roadside food joints with a nonchalance that was signature to predators.

The evening light had begun to fade when the vehicle slowed down by a children's park. The lane conjoining the park was packed with cars that had arrived to pick up the children and take them back to the safety of their homes. The van glided past the lane and turned into another one, only to return a little later.

Dusk had now determinedly descended. A few stragglers remained in the lane. A little girl – she appeared to be around seven – hopped along the curb, occasionally running in circles around her maid, who was on the phone. They appeared to be waiting for someone to pick them up.

The van came slowly to a halt taking the place of a fruit-seller, a regular outside the park, who had packed up for the day and had started to push his cart out of the lane.

The child started to play hopscotch. Her hair, tied up in two ponytails, bounced along with her. Hop, 1-2-3, hop.

The maid called out to her to stay close, but the child was determined to reach the far end of her imaginary hopscotch matrix. The maid went back to her call.

The road was now empty. The child jumped on the last two numbers of the grid. The van jump-started. Tyres screeched, and in a matter of seconds it was over, leaving the horrified maid with no time to react; by the time she understood what had happened, the child and the van were gone.

***

Across the city, a man sat in a restaurant, waiting for what he anticipated would be a hopelessly prickly meeting to begin. He had chosen a place she loved, a popular pizza joint at a street corner that looked out at the ocean. They'd had numerous meetings at this spot, discussing how deep, how wide, how fathomless the ocean could be.

Of course, the pizza place hadn't been around then. Nor the people who made them. Good days, he thought gloomily.

He scrutinised the elaborate menu with distaste – 'Sex on the Beach', 'Blue Lagoon', 'Peaches and scream'... What was all this balderdash? What happened to the good ol'-fashioned single malt? Humans had evolved to be needlessly complicated, something he had been blindsided by, considering their superior intelligence.

*That's exactly why*, she'd say.

He sighed. This was going to go badly no matter how many beers he got her to down. Or cups of tea. These were the only two human innovations she approved of. He knew she especially enjoyed the latter in bed, first thing in the morning, when her hair fell around her in waves, framing her face like the sun. She had always acknowledged he could fashion a mean bed tea.

He rubbed his eyes. How was he going to do this?

The air in the room shifted in a heady ripple. She was here.

A woman entered the restaurant. She wore an elegant, hand-woven, golden and peach linen saree with tiny embroidered flowers scattered across the pallu. As she made her way towards him, people stared unabashedly. Not just because she was gorgeous, but because they could not understand the way she seemed to know each one of them – not as an acquaintance, but with a knowledge so much deeper. Her eyes were arresting, holding them down in a deep knowing; bristling with a life that they had yet to live, that they wanted, were waiting for. The fragrance of the forest and wet earth lingered after she moved past them. She seemed to know everything, and that seemed impossible. Just like it was impossible that red and copper highlights seemed to travel the length of her hair, as if catching the light with a fiery determination long after the sun had gone down.

He stood up to welcome her. Unlike the others in the café, he could see her true self. Beautiful, but terrifying. Her eyes, which were usually pools of gentle rivers, were reminiscent of stormy seas. Her body was like a shifting canvas, at times enveloped by gnarled roots, at others by clusters of rainforest canopies.

Mahi. The earth.

The fragrance that the others smelled did not greet him. He smelled blood, and fire and rotting sewage. He was met by an icy draft that would have frozen his soul had he possessed one.

She was angry.

He passed her the cocktail menu, 'What shall we drink to?'

She ignored it, poised her long fingers over her glass and filled it with water.

'I don't have time for small talk, Sangatarash.' Her voice was deep and guttural, a lot like his own. 'Get to the point.'

He took a deep breath, wounded by her uncharacteristic hostility. 'Management is a bit worried, Mahi.' Well, the 'bit worried' was an understatement, he told himself. Heads were rolling all over the offices.

'About?' She looked to the waiter, who scrambled past several heads to get to her side.

'Tea, please,' she smiled, and he left, disappointed that she had not asked him for a vital organ.

She turned to Sangatarash and asked slowly. 'About?'

'The children, Mahi.'

\*\*\*

The van stopped at a dilapidated warehouse. It wasn't on the outskirts of the city, or far away from it. It was just a few turns away from a busy suburb. This is the thing with large cities that never sleep. They are full of places where few people go and even fewer register. Places where crimes are committed, where the absolute chaos of a metropolis buries any screams without a single witness.

Three men climbed out of the front and opened the double doors of the van. The large compound was quiet, a few old bulbs straining to step in for the almost-faded light.

The child was sitting deep inside, a gag over her mouth, hands tied in front of her. She was trembling.

'Come on out, we won't hurt you,' said one of the men, reaching forward.

She recoiled, leaning away as much as she could, and started to whimper.

'Hurry this up. I don't want anyone listening to this,' said the man who had been driving the van, and clearly the leader of the group.

The two others reached inside and forcefully pulled the little form from the van. As she slid to the edge of the van, she kicked out at their faces, and as they scattered, startled, launched herself into the street and took off running at a speed that seemed impossible for her size. She rounded a corner and turned into one of the narrow deserted lanes of the crumbling mill compound. The two men recovered quickly and took off behind her. A light rain began to fall over the compound.

\*\*\*

He watched the rain come down, making abstract art on the windows from the traffic lights outside. It was unseasonal, this sudden shower, and he knew she'd done it just to piss him off. Especially since he was wearing an expensive suit.

She smiled as if she'd read his mind. She couldn't really, but she knew him well enough to make an assumption. It wasn't a pleasant smile.

Sangatarash sighed. 'It's *exactly* stuff like this that's upsetting the management. Rain, tornadoes, fires – all your elements have gone rogue – and now these children. You need to stop this, Mahi.'

'Or else?' Flames ringed her pupils.

'Mahi, just try and under – '

'Or *else*, Sanga?'

He stopped short at her nickname for him. Sanga, short for Sangatarash, the sculptor, mason, the evolutionary. Only she called him that.

'They'll strip you of your powers, Mahi,' he continued wearily. 'You are a part of a system, a universe. You cannot do as you please.'

'And you can?' Her whole body seemed to emanate the heat from her eyes. She was all volcanoes, hard corners and jagged edges.

'Didn't you do exactly as you pleased to me, Sanga? We were in this together. We started to build all this together. You're the fucking Head of Evolution. Your responsibility towards me, towards all your planets, was paramount! Look what your humans are doing to each other, to me. I am hotter than ever before, and not in a good way, mind you.'

'They're your humans too, Mahi.'

'Not any more. They were, maybe at some point. Now, they are attacking each other, me, and they're raping babies. BABIES, Sanga! Out of a misplaced sense of power, out of a sense of entitlement. They are not human anymore. And so they're no longer mine.'

'And the children? What about the children, Mahi?'

Her eyes turned to stone. 'You left me no choice.'

***

The men turned the corner and stopped short. The child was standing in the middle of the deserted lane, facing them. Something about her stance gave them pause. She seemed unnaturally quiet. Unmoving. Still.

The shutters along the pavement were all downed, the graffiti on them old and worn, screaming causes and jokes long forgotten. The rain was investigating every crevice, puncturing the mist to reach every closed window of the buildings that were stacked impossibly close together. It drummed down on the little girl wearing a creased frock with a bow that had come undone at the back. She reached towards her mouth, and seemed to be working on the gag. It came loose and fell to the ground.

The men immediately moved forward, but she did not even flinch. As they inched closer, they heard a deep rumbling.

They exchanged glances. 'Dogs, maybe. Let's just grab her and run,' said one of them, voicing the thoughts of his companions.

They sprinted towards her, registering how still she was, how she just stood there, staring at them fixedly.

It only dawned on them when they got right up to her that the sound was coming from her. The girl was growling.

They looked at each other, befuddled, uncertain.

'Ay, stop that,' one of the men said.

She turned a blank, unseeing gaze towards him, and her mouth stretched into a smile. Except, it wasn't exactly a smile. It sent a shiver down his spine.

He staggered backwards. *What the fuck was happening to this kid?*

Thunder rolled across the skies, and the men shivered; they knew it was not from the cold. She growled again, a low, raspy rumble coming from deep within, and they heard rage and hatred in the sound. It seemed to radiate from her. Were her eyes different? They couldn't tell in the rain.

'What the fuck are you guys doing?'

The men jumped in shock at the sound of their leader's voice behind them. The child stood her ground. The third man jogged up to them and grabbed her arm roughly. What happened next was a blur. The girl snarled angrily, bared her teeth to reveal fangs and clamped them down on the man's arm, slicing it clean in half. He screamed in agony as he fell to the ground writhing, blood springing from the stump that was once his arm. His men stood around paralysed, until one of them let out a yelp of horror. The girl still did not move, blood dripping from her jaw to her chin and onto the road.

The men tried to help their injured leader up, and just as they started to drag him away, she giggled. The sound echoed around the street. They looked back at her. She brought her hands to her mouth, and tore off the rope that held her hands captive. She giggled again, her chubby palms held over the mouth, like a child that had been caught doing something she wasn't supposed to. The sight of her made their flesh crawl. When she met their gaze, she stopped, her face suddenly deadpan. Then she threw her head back and howled into the night. The men dropped their leader in terror, as the child sounded howl after howl, rain dripping from her hair, blood dribbling off her chin and onto the rainy street. They started to run, but she was faster. In seconds, she was upon them, her baby weight wrapped around their shoulders. She reached out and slashed at their throats with claws they could have sworn weren't there, until they were. The last thing they saw as they sputtered to death in a puddle of red, was the sight of her tiny form hop-scotching away from them.

*\*\**

She took a sip of her tea as if it was the only thing that mattered in the world. She was ignoring him. He sighed and placed a bunch of newspapers in front of her. Headlines screamed out triumphantly from the pages: 'Kidnappers Found with Slashed Throats, Children Unable to Explain What Happened', 'Rapists Found Burnt to Death by Woman, Witnesses Claim She Used Nothing But Her Eyes', 'Who's the Weaker Sex Now?'

She cringed. 'Such terrible writing,' she sniffed.

'Mahi, call this off. Come and meet the board.'

'No.'

'No?'

'No. And don't threaten me about what I can and cannot do, Sanga. I'll fucking sneeze and the planet as you know it, me, everything you've worked so hard for – it'll all be gone. One sneeze.'

Sangatarash flinched at the memory. It was 65 million years ago, but crystal clear in his mind. They were watching the last of the dinosaurs go. Crying and laughing about what they'd built and what they'd had to let go off.

'What about me,' she'd asked him playfully as they sat enveloped in a comfortable hug, looking out at the vast landscape. 'What if I had to leave? How would I do it? With a big bang, just as I was made?'

'Ah, no,' he'd said, 'how pedestrian. For you, it should be something phenomenal. Something big, like a…like a sneeze.'

She'd giggled. 'So if I wanted to reboot, I'd just…sneeze?'

'Yes, so be it.'

'You're so strange, Sanga,' she laughed. 'What would I reboot as?'

'As atoms, Mahi, as beautiful, free atoms, that would come together to form...you. Because the universe can't handle too many Mahis. Just one is enough.'

She'd mock-punched him. 'Damn straight, Sanga...'

You know I'll do it.' Her low firm voice swung him back to the present. She wasn't looking at him. She was watching the rain.

'You'd end it all? Just like that? After all this time?'

'Four and a half billion years, to be exact,' she said, turning to face him. 'And yes, in a heartbeat. I'm *that* done.' Creepers comfortingly encircled her wrists as she continued to sip her tea.

For onlookers this was still very much a pleasant dinner between two magnetic, if slightly strange, people. They couldn't hear the raised voices, the strange changes that appeared on her body, nothing.

'Mahi, there's no need for extreme steps like that. Let's talk about this.'

Her expression turned from shock to rage. 'Talk? I tried to talk about it, Sanga. I tried to talk about it when your team suggested the creation of this race. I trusted you. And I welcomed them.

'I tried to talk about it when you decided they would have the sort of brainpower that will help everything I hold dear. That will HELP the way I function.

'I tried to talk about it when their superior intelligence started to give rise to negative emotions, to power, greed, entitlement that started to cause problems for everything else I am responsible for.

'I tried to talk about it when you decided NOT to abort when they started to attack each other, because the scientist in you wanted to 'see how this goes'!' she almost spat out the last bit.

The rain beat down outside now, the horizon was lost from view. Lightning streaked across the sky followed by the roar of an angry thunder.

He jumped at the loud crack. 'I was trying to find what worked! I'm in charge of evolution, Mahi, my very job is to ensure things grow. I tried something new...'

'And IT FAILED, Sanga,' she cried. 'And it's hurting everything we built.

She took his hand in hers, and the warmth of her touch made him ache. 'Life took what it needed, preyed for food, reproduced for offspring and some, like humans, mated for pleasure. When we created life, it was never meant to plunder and loot. You taught me that. You said nothing is wasted in nature and everything has a purpose. We gave every creature, all life, the ability to protect itself. Speed, camouflage, roots, flight... But there is no protection against this. Against rape. Which means it was never meant to happen, was it?'

He looked away, tried to pull his hand away. She held on tighter.

'You can admit it to me, Sanga. This is a flaw in your system.'

He pulled away, uncomfortable and agitated. People were starting to stare. She pressed on.

'But this, this is rape of the natural world as we knew it.'

He pursed his lips, continued to look away.

She tried to take his hand again. 'You should fix what you fucked up. Admit that you did, Sanga!'

'Yes, *fine*, I FUCKED UP,' he exploded, slapping his hand on the table. 'But what now? You'll do my job? This is my work you're messing with. You don't even know what you're doing. You're passing animal strengths to some humans, the strength of your elements to others. You cannot randomly mess with the balance. And what about the children? In some ways they're monsters now. Half human, half animal. How will they grow up like this? Have you considered the damage this will do to them?'

She laughed without humour. 'This will do damage, but being raped while they're babies will not? I say let the damage come from the power to protect themselves rather than the consequences of some entitled demons! As for what will happen to them, I'll figure the kinks out. We'll *evolve*,' she said cruelly.

She paused, debating over telling him more. Then she sighed and said, 'Also, they're not alone.'

*\*\*\**

The child was bawling in the street now, disoriented, walking slowly to the van again, unable to understand what had happened, what she had done. The blood on her clothes scared her, and she cried out for her mother. The street remained empty, not a soul could hear her.

Except for the three women who came looking for her. She'd never seen them before but knew instinctively that they were alike. She ran to them, sobs wracking her tiny body as they enveloped her in a protective hug.

'It's okay, it's okay. We're here now.'

They wrapped her up in dry towels and walked to their car. 'Let's take you to your mumma, little one.'

*\*\*\**

They'd been sitting in silence for a while now. The restaurant was almost empty.

They looked at each other. Of all the planets that he'd planned, she was his masterpiece. He had put in centuries of work with her, fallen in love with her, delighted in her creations, mourned their extinctions, taken the harsh decisions he had to and, for the most part, they had agreed; together they had been unstoppable. Then he'd created humans.

'What do you want, Mahi?'

She shrugged. 'A do-over. We've been through five mass extinctions together, Sanga. Maybe it's time for the sixth. Let's bring back the humans when you have a better plan. They are extraordinary creatures, but you'll need a version 2.0.'

He shook his head. 'I can't do that. I've been told to work with this. We cannot let the last 200,000 years of work be wiped off like this. Let me fix the glitches. Let me see what I can do to change them.'

'How will you change them,' she asked.

'What do you mean, I'll check the issues and – '

'No, I mean, what will you change specifically?'

He stayed silent.

'The papers are full of attacks on my creations. Did you know, Sanga, the humans want to build a 600 foot statue on a river bank so they're shifting 300 – not 20, not 30, mind you – but 300 crocodiles to a place that's not their natural habitat? Ecological balance aside, these are animals with homing tendencies! They'll come back. Do you know what will happen when they return to find their home encroached, teeming with humans? Can you live with the consequences of that?'

Sanga shook his head. Mahi stormed on angrily.

'Yesterday, a group of men raped a six year old at a railway station,' her voice broke at this, but she wiped her tears angrily. 'A baby, Sanga. Will you change this part of them? Or will you tackle their commentary on what everyone else — man, woman, or otherwise — should wear, not wear, how they should live, eat, walk? What will you change, Sanga?'

Her anger stretched over and above her, her body flashing with betrayal and hurt. The wind howled and thunder bellowed its dissent. The ocean outside swelled and lashed out with an enormous wave that crashed on the shore.

He turned to the screams of panic of the passers-by as they scattered to escape the water. 'Easy, Mahi, stop that.'

'No,' she said. 'I shan't. I don't want these children. It's my choice, not yours. I don't want them. You fucked this up, Sanga. You owe me this.'

He looked back at her. There was something broken about her, today. They'd argued before, but this was different. She had distanced herself from him eons ago because of this very argument. It had torn them apart. She wanted to have nothing to do with him or the management. They'd pushed her too far. She was right. Of course she was right. It was the rape of the natural world. Of her.

And, yet, he had orders. He collected himself. It was time to take the harsh decisions he was known for.

He looked down at the table, unable to look her in the eye. 'I'm sorry, Mahi, since you're not ready to comply, we'll have to take away your powers. The elements will be temporarily assigned to me, the animals, everything.'

They stared at each other for what seemed like eternity.

'We did good for a while there, Sanga,' she said, a curious emotion coating her voice. 'And we will again, some day.'

He started. 'What does that mean?'

'Try and do better by me next time, Sanga. And even if you don't, I'll manage. I was fine before you, and I'll be fine after you.'

She took a tissue from the rack on the table.

'Mahi, *don't*.' He lunged towards her.

'Tell the big boys upstairs that I quit.'

She sneezed.

# TRIDEVI TURBULENCE

## TRISHA DAS

'It's called *Tri*-devi for a reason,' Parvati's red and gold eyes flashed haughtily from under her lowered lashes as she perched on a bench of ice at the peak of Mount Everest. Her chin was pushed up as usual, her lower lip jutting out just the slightest bit – it was the look she got when she didn't want to do something. 'There can only be three in a triumvirate, Ganga.'

An aircraft circled loudly over their heads for the seventh time that morning, giving another group of twenty-four mortals the legitimate opportunity to post an airplane-window-selfie with the hashtags #MtEverest, #OnceInALifetime #Wanderlust on their social media profiles. Parvati frowned in annoyance and waved a finger at the plane – it spiralled out of control for a few moments, probably scaring the bejesus out of the mortals inside. There'd be twenty-four new #Survivor posts within the hour.

'Then we can call it a quadrumvirate,' replied Ganga in as reasonable a voice as she could muster while trying her best to stay still and not bob side to side on her watery stomach and betray her nervousness. Her feet were still anchored by Shiva's matted locks a few hundred kilometres away on Mount Kailash – a situation that remained unchanged despite Parvati's best efforts. Ganga had got quite used to leaning. In more ways than one.

Parvati blinked and looked away into the distance and back towards her home on Mount Kailash, where she knew her recalcitrant husband, Shiva, was meditating. He probably hadn't even noticed that she'd flown off in a huff after he'd smiled at one of Ganga's antics. Parvati had left slowly, and noisily, in the hope that he'd open his eyes (the regular ones) and notice that his consort was upset with him. His beloved consort. His *only* consort. She refused to call that flirtatious squatter that had fallen into his hair from the heavens a consort. Parasite would be a more accurate description. 'There are only three gods in the Trimurti, Ganga. You need to have an equal number of consorts in the Tridevi.'

Ganga tilted her head with a swooshy ripple, 'Fine, then I could take your place. Lakshmi, Saraswati and I. As your older sister, shouldn't I have precedence? After all, I'm the one Shiva loves.'

'You,' Parvati's tone was acerbic, 'are *not* the one he loves.' A humming started as another airplane approached the mountain. She waved her finger again in irritation, bringing on a massive blizzard that enveloped the peak. The plane turned around immediately.

'I think Shiva would disagree. He considers me as much his companion as you,' said Ganga, calmly diverting an avalanche with a tsunami-like wave of her body. There was a group of mountain-climbers below that didn't deserve to die because her sister was perpetually in a bad mood.

It was a sticky point, and Parvati knew it. After all, Ganga's residence in Shiva's hair was entirely official and, despite all the hype about his self-control, her husband had eventually succumbed to Ganga's charms after pretending to resist her for what felt like all of five minutes. Just like he'd succumbed to Parvati's wiles to get him to marry her. There was a reason why mortal men worshipped her husband's penis, she thought snarkily.

'Also,' Ganga continued, 'I'm the only goddess who has been, in a sense, a consort to all three in the Trimurti. I flow from Vishnu's feet into Brahma's water pot and fall to earth from Shiva's head. If anything, I should take precedence over all three of you.'

A snort sounded loudly in the air around them, sending a flock of golden birds fluttering out of a cloud.

Parvati sighed, 'Show yourself, Lakshmi.'

The blizzard clouds in front of them parted and Lakshmi, dressed in red athleisure wear and clutching a smartphone, flew towards them, leaving a trail of diamond solitaires in the wind behind her. She didn't take her eyes off the phone to greet them but that wasn't what had both the goddesses looking on widening their eyes in surprise.

'Er, Lakshmi?' ventured Ganga.

'Hmmm?'

'Have you…put on some weight?'

This made Lakshmi look up. The folds on her body had indeed multiplied since they had last met. Morbidly so. She flicked her phone to standby, carved herself an extra-large platinum throne out of the ice with a wave of her finger and asked as she settled into it with an uncomfortable wheeze, 'Have I?'

'You have,' said Parvati with a fair bit of disdain, her back bone straightening with subtle pride for her rather emaciated figure. Ribs strained against her skin beneath small, naked breasts and her midnight complexion glowed with even more stars than usual.

Lakshmi shrugged, 'Maybe a little. But I own it, so it doesn't matter. Besides, Vishnu doesn't mind.' She ran her finger absently over the ice next to her throne and it turned into Italian marble.

Now it was Ganga's turn to snort. A river-rapid flowed from her throat as she did so.

Lakshmi turned on her with a slightly malevolent look. 'Just because you flow from my husband's feet, doesn't make you his consort.'

Parvati nodded emphatically, 'That's exactly what I'm trying to tell her!'

Ganga rolled her eyes, 'You two are so insecure. Saraswati agrees with me.'

'No, she doesn't,' Parvati and Lakshmi said at the same time. Lakshmi blinked uncertainly and gold coins fell from her eyes.

'Does too.' Ganga's arms crossed over her chest with a giant splash. The truth was, she didn't know. Saraswati had certainly made all the right noises when Ganga had complained about how Parvati got all the importance while she herself was left largely unrecognized as Shiva's companion in the mortal world. Now that Shiva worship had reduced even more among the mortals and politically correct Vishnu was having his time in the sun, Ganga had been relegated to little more than a dustbin for mankind's waste. Perhaps, she had explained to Saraswati, if she were given a bit more respect and recognition, if she were a principal goddess within the triumvirate of principal goddesses, she would be left untainted by the mortals enough to complete her earthly journey with some semblance of dignity instead of carrying and dumping an entire country's filth into the ocean every day. Most of the creatures that had thrived within her waters for millennia were dead, her clear pink colour had turned to a blotchy brown-grey, and the stench of decay and death never left her. She was exhausted of it all, she'd told Saraswati as she crashed her arms about in enormous waves. It was time to change the way things were done.

'Besides,' mumbled Parvati with a sneer, bringing Ganga back to the discussion at hand, 'Saraswati's opinion barely matters anymore.'

'I heard that.'

Saraswati walked up to them barefoot and unadorned, appearing out of the tempestuous air. She looked old and haggard. Her normally white saree was tattered and had large saffron-coloured stains on it. She caught the others looking and sighed, 'I know. Don't ask.' Her despair hung like a wrung-out shroud around her.

They waited for her to sit on the ice before Ganga asked, 'Saraswati, do you think it's unreasonable for me to be considered Brahma's consort? I do, after all, flow into his water-pot and am always with him.'

Saraswati shrugged, 'If you can make him bestir himself enough to realize he even has a consort, you're welcome to him.'

Lakshmi made a sarcastic attempt at sympathy, 'Is the poor thing still depressed?'

Saraswati looked Lakshmi up and down with a frown as she replied, 'Dearest sister, not everyone can be as *prosperous* as you and your husband are these days.'

Ganga flowed over in a show of support but only ended up getting Saraswati's saree wet. The saffron colour leaked a bit into Ganga's own watery depths as she sighed into Saraswati's limp hair, 'Times are hard, I know.'

A tinge of wetness, whether from Ganga or independent of her, filmed over Saraswati's eyes. 'The very worst since he made the beginning. I don't know what to do. He's just barely hanging on by the skin of his teeth.' A wrinkled lotus petal fell from her eye on to her lap.

Parvati shivered a little, and not because she was naked. Times hadn't exactly been peachy for Shiva either and, as his consort, they were even worse for her. Shiva had once been the most powerful god in the Trimurti. They had, as a couple, enjoyed the attention and devotion of mortals almost exclusively for a long time. But, of late, Vishnu got most of the glory while Shiva came a slow second and Brahma was almost entirely out of the race. She needed to get Shiva back on top. Things were on a slippery slope and Saraswati's condition was testament to how bad it could be if she didn't keep pushing to stay relevant. Ganga's quest to replace her in the Tridevi could jeopardize not only her influence, but Shiva's as well. The idea of a principal god coupled with a mere river goddess – it was ridiculous!

'As the most senior of us all...' Parvati ignored the disagreement on all three faces and continued, 'I'd like to share my opinion.'

She looked at Saraswati, 'Mortals are weak-willed, self-serving creatures. You have to give them what they want. You and your husband didn't move with the times and you became irrelevant. Don't ask them to strive higher, or be any better than their base selves. Just give them what they want.'

Saraswati looked at Parvati and replied in an even voice, 'Like you and Shiva did? You gave mortals everything they wanted and now even you've lost your hold on them. Unbridled lust, drug-filled orgies, bloody carnage – it's no wonder that mortals turned into walking vats of guilt. It is staid old Vishnu, who has never had a moment of fun except when he fornicated with sixteen thousand mortal women as Krishna, who has won in the end.'

Lakshmi's expression struggled between glee at her husband being acknowledged as the most powerful god in the Trimurti and irritation at the thought of him fornicating with sixteen thousand women.

'It need not be the end for Shiva,' piped up Ganga, refusing to let go of her own agenda. 'Maybe all that is needed is a change of scenery. Let's face it – Parvati's time as his consort has been a bit…intense.'

At that, Parvati began to lose her temper and look like red-tongued, demon-skull-clad Kali instead. Ganga wasn't intimidated. She pointed at Kali and said, 'See? Too intense. Maybe it's time for a more family-friendly image for Shiva.'

Kali screamed and began to dance in fury. Blood and fire flew everywhere. The mountain trembled and the heavens flashed. A massive quake rocked the earth beneath her. She roared and grunted, grew a thousand times bigger and then roared and grunted some more. It was a spectacular, apocalyptic sight.

Ganga, Lakshmi and Saraswati sat, sedate and unimpressed, waiting for her to calm down.

Finally, Kali brought down a massive ball of fire on Ganga. It washed away easily in her waters as she grew to the same size as Kali, looked her in the eye and said nonchalantly, 'Are you done with your little tantrum?'

Kali's red eyes met Ganga's blue ones, and blinked. Then, in an instant, she was regular-sized Parvati again, sitting with the others on the blizzardy mountain-top, sighing to herself.

Ganga receded gently, but her eyes were angry, 'Okay, look, I'm going to level with the three of you. I actually have no desire to be part of your precious little Tridevi club. What I want, what I *need*, is to either be shown some respect on earth or to just go back to heaven, where I can flow in peace. I can't go on like this. I'm getting dirtier and smellier by the day. Even Shiva is beginning to notice and, let's face it, he doesn't exactly smell like roses himself.'

Parvati's eyes lit up, 'So go back to heaven then.' It was the perfect solution. Two birds with one stone.

'I can't,' cried Ganga in frustration, 'I spoke to both Shiva and Vishnu. There was no point speaking to Brahma. No offence, Saraswati.'

'None taken.'

Ganga's sigh rippled outwards, 'They refused. They're both perfectly happy to, ahem, dip into my waters regularly. They don't want things to change.'

Lakshmi exclaimed, 'Vishnu does not dip into your water!'

Ganga gave her the eye, 'Yes, he does. And not just his feet.'

Lakshmi glared at her.

Parvati decided to ignore the exchange and instead asked plaintively, 'What did Shiva say about your taking my place in the Tridevi?'

'He told me to speak to you about it.'

Parvati rolled her eyes, 'Typical.'

Saraswati shook her head, 'It's impossible to expect them to do anything about it. Gods made men in their image and, unfortunately, that means that they will take advantage of you, just like mortals would. You must take control of your own destiny, Ganga.'

'How?'

Saraswati thought about it for a moment, 'Dry up, like I did.' She had been a river on earth at one time too. 'If your water is the only thing about your situation you can actually control, then give up your water. Let both god and mortal try to cope without your sustenance. It would take a little time but, once you've dried, you can return to heaven in peace.'

Ganga considered it and then said, 'But, if I'm not a river, I won't be worshipped or considered a goddess anymore. And if I'm not a goddess then what will I be?'

Saraswati chuckled, 'Free?'

Ganga sloshed backwards a few paces and gazed upon her companions – the principal goddesses that formed the Tridevi. Bad-tempered Parvati, fat Lakshmi and worn-out Saraswati. She smiled.

'Free.'

The others watched as Ganga's smile slowly widened into a grin. She turned and waved over her shoulder as her waters raged in a flood towards Mount Kailash. When she'd disappeared, the Tridevi looked at each other with pensive expressions. After a few agonizing moments of silence, Parvati said aloud what they were all thinking, 'I wouldn't mind being free either.'

*(The river Ganga is, indeed, drying up due to global warming and the endemic abuse of 500 million people. There will come a time when, like the Saraswati, it will only exist in mythology.)*

# STONE COLD

## KIRAN MANRAL

The moonlight was cold on her skin. The door, a massive, ponderous structure of wood, the one she guarded with him, was now shut. Their day's work was done. Not much happened inside the building now anyway — it was good only for decay and disuse.

Outside the gate, the city waited for her, quiet, coiled and tense with the uncertainty of the darkness that followed the briskness of the day. She looked over at the road beyond the barbed wire on the shelled-out compound wall that kept the city out of this now derelict, sacrosanct site that held the wealth of the nation. On the other side of the massive door stood her brother, his undefined features contorting themselves into a yawn, awake for his nightly sojourn into the land of the mortals. He was ugly, with a protruding belly, and held on to his money bag with all his might. They were a contrast to each other, perhaps created that way — one to seduce with the gentleness of beauty, and the other to enslave with the arrogance of wealth.

Above them, a gibbous moon smiled through a swiftly streaming lattice of clouds beyond the Dome. An occasional star dared to twinkle through the carpet of smog that hung low over the horizon beyond. The pole star was nowhere to be seen, the crispness of the million fires across the city streamed upwards, towards a disinterested heaven. Citizens burnt their waste in symbolic bonfires every weekend, reminding themselves they were just as temporary and destructible. Only the Brotherhood was permanent.

The smoke from the bonfires would be filtered out through thousands of suction pipes embedded in the Dome. Freshly manufactured air would be pumped in, air infused with predetermined gases that kept the citizens alert during the day and sent them into somnabulence as night fell. These gases didn't affect her. She was stone made flesh, and then made back to stone again.

The man who made her, with his unruly hair, crumpled face and kindly eyes, was long gone. He was perhaps the only man who had ever looked at her as stone and seen her in the flesh. To the rest of the world, she was just a sculpture, cold, monolithic, unresponsive. But he knew she existed in flesh and spirit beneath the stone carved out from the Baijnath mountains. Hacked out and transported first by narrow gauge and then broad gauge down to the plains, to the city. He had watched her come to life as careful hands had carved her from the squat stone, and gave her a face and a form.

The men who had carved her were from a place that was then called Guntur, in a state called Andhra Pradesh, 13 of them, under the guidance of the tousled-haired, kind-eyed artist. Their families had carved statues for centuries, and knowing how to make stone sing and curve it into form and flesh was in their blood. Now, of course, there was no ornamentation. No sculpture. No art. No music. No literature. Nothing to feed the mind other than what the Brotherhood approved of. Worthless pursuits, the Brotherhood called them, and did not encourage their existence.

Those 13 men had put her together piece by piece. Twenty-one feet high. Four stone pieces. She was joined together, head, neck, shoulder, belly, knee, foot. Each piece weighed 15 tonnes. She was magnificent when they were done with her, but she was doomed to never see her own magnificence. She stood unnoticed by most who used to enter the gates. They were always in a hurry, their movements hastened by the lack of time, the urgency of appointments to be kept, queues to be stood in, tasks to be finished. Humans and their obsession with time. Didn't they know that they had enough of it, and it never ended? It only kept stretching itself out into a cyclical loop that spun through the fabric of space-time. Perhaps they didn't. But she did. She sighed. It was so wearisome to count time in these minuscule human fragments. A blink of an eye to a god, a lifetime for a human being.

For centuries she had stood here, guarding the door of this repository of wealth, through the searing heat of the summer, the numbing cold of winter, holding in her hands a flower and paddy cluster, the emblems of prosperity. But, sometimes, she vacated her post; on some nights she slipped into skin.

****

Diksha stood in line for the phosphorescent graphic to be stamped on her wrist, allowing her entry into the club. The music was so loud that she felt it burn a hole through her eardrums, shredding the delicate membrane to tatters and rattling the three little bones within, that tap tapped their message into the cochlea. Incus, malleus, stapes. Hammer, anvil, stirrup. Some forgotten recesses of her brain dredged up an old lesson from the eighth standard, about ancient human anatomy, from the millennia before the Change.

Nothing had been the same after the Change, the tipping of the Earth's axis, leading to a cataclysm on the surface. Those who survived kept getting retreaded, like tyres,. Body parts replaced, cells rewired, devices inserted, kept functional by technology and chemicals. Most of the pure humans left were a precious species, protected by the Brotherhood, segregated, kept eternally. The rest were cyborgs, part human and part robot, created with a purpose, working till they wore out because a new batch could always be created. And then there were the Pure. Cloned from select humans, genetically engineered to fit the new norms of aesthetics, made to adapt to any kind of planetary surface, just in case they needed to exit Earth in a hurry.

She was one of the Pure. Born of genetic splicing and implantation into a human womb, and handed over to the CareCyborgs when she was removed from it. She was created for a purpose. She was among the few who were the future of humankind.

Next to her, Aman was rocking on his heels, his eyes zoned out, which could only mean that he was high again. She shook her head. 'Listen, you've got to drive us back home – you're not going to drink, okay,' she yelled into his ear. 'I'll call you when I'm ready to leave.'

He nodded, his eyes still focused on something she could not see. They trundled into the flashing dimness of the club. The crowd engulfed them as they spilled in – the friends, the acquaintances, the noise, the bonhomie. Gove, the one who took charge of forbidden supplies, raised an enquiring brow at her. She shook her head; no substance today, perhaps some shots later. It exhausted her. In fact, all of it tired her. This group, this determination to make merry, to be hedonistic in a world where hedonism was forbidden. Any gatherings other than rallies for the Brotherhood were banned. This was underground, where the drones couldn't track them. On the surface, below the Dome, they were constantly monitored, the trackers implanted in the back of their necks pinpointing where they were at every given moment to the Keepers of the Brotherhood. Within the Dome, millions of tiny eyes beamed back all human activity to the distant control room in the reconnaissance headquarters of the Motherland. Somewhere in those dank cement bunkers, miles below the surface of the earth, the heart and internal organs of the Brotherhood fed off the infinite lives and loves playing out on the datastreams that gave them sustenance

There was no hiding on the surface. There were lights in every corner, and you knew you were being watched. But you figured out how to get around it. With a duplicate chip available in the black market that you could activate on the nights you wanted to go underground. Diksha had deactivated her original one with the help of a hacking device that allowed the chip to still show as 'active' in the system. She had then activated the duplicate chip, to be valid for eight hours of escape, once a month. She had paid a fortune in food credits for it. To the Brotherhood, she was asleep now, in her compact bed, back in her cell at the Centre for the Pure. If they ever found out that she was one among the Rebels, her ambition to become among the first women to be inducted into the Brotherhood would be doomed. She knew that. But her need to defy the constricting system battled fiercely with her desire for power – and, more often than not, the defiant side won. But in reality here she was, inside the dark dank space of an old, disused building, the stairway crisscrossed with deflecting sonic waves acting as a sonar fence. They were as safe as they could be. Drone eyes could not penetrate this space, the trackers couldn't track them. The ones who visited here were protected. But just for a while. Until they went out again through the octopus-like tunnels that led out from the discotheque into a warren of tightly packed neighbourhoods. Tunnels that were locked behind wardrobes and which opened only on nights on which the whisper network unlocked them, and the homes they led into emptied themselves of their decoy occupants to let the revellers escape.

She stepped onto the dance floor, feeling the music work its way through her skin, her muscles, her bones, her body moving of its own accord, her heart pounding in symphony with the beat. She was beautiful when she danced – she knew that. The floor cleared a bit for her, and then some more. A woman came through the crowd, a stranger. Diksha had seen her here before. She was different in a way that no one was these days, full-bodied with high round breasts and broad hips that seemed to move on their own. The regulation body suit she wore stretched dangerously as she walked, taut to the point of splitting itself. Diksha noticed the gaze of the men shifting from her to the woman. They stood around, watching her, their eyes dilating, the lust she aroused in them something they could not explain or control anymore than they could stop themselves from watching her. She looked around the gathered ring of men like gladiators bristling for combat, their breathing heavy and ragged from desire, and her eyes fixed on Diksha. They were heavy-lidded, almond-shaped, Diksha noticed, as their eyes locked. A hint of a smile appeared on the woman's face. Just as Diksha was about to take a step forward, a man pushed her aside and strode up to the woman. He began dancing with her, his movements jerky and uncoordinated, dissonant with naked desire.

Diksha watched on from the fringe of the dance floor, fascinated by this strange woman, her skin the colour of molten gold. Who was she, where had she come from, why was she so different from the rest of them? Hour-glass. That's what they used to call the shape of this woman's body, the shape that women aspired to before the accepted aesthetic demanded tall, androgynous bodies. Those hips, the wide, child-bearing hips required for the bones of the pelvis to separate and allow the head of the offspring to pass through the birth canal. But women didn't bear children anymore. They had no need of such hips. They needed to be, like the men, lean and highly effective, strong and totally without desire. Only those without desire or those who had no fornication transgressions against them were selected for positions in the Brotherhood. The rest were Workers.

The woman moved with the man who had approached her on the dance floor, her body a groundswell of want and yearning, exuding promise and fulfilment. Then, just like that, the lights went off for a second and they both disappeared. The crowd looked around, startled for a moment, snapped out of the trance she seemed to have drawn them into. 'They must have gone into a pod,' one of the onlookers muttered, and went back to moving in a desultory manner on the dance floor. The music pulsated on, the DJ spun his tracks, the bar got crowded, people came in and went out in waves of bodies, but all the energy had now been vacuumed out of the space.

'Who was she?' Diksha asked Gove, who was busy fondling the breast of girl he'd just been introduced to a few seconds ago, while she stuck her tongue deep enough down his throat to induce asphyxiation if left there for more than a few seconds.

He detached himself long enough from the girl to reply, 'No clue,' and went back to making out.

'Get a pod, you guys,' she said in disgust and went off to find Aman. She wanted to leave, the music was doing nothing for her tonight, nor were the shots. The lights pulsated with the music, dimming and brightening, lighting up and darkening faces every alternate second. The crowd pressed around her, making her breathless and panicky. She stumbled in the surge and ebb of the crowd. A hand reached out and propped her up. It was the woman from the dance floor. Standing at the side of the stairway, a lit cigarette in one hand, her other hand on Diksha's wrist where she'd grabbed her. Her touch was cool, ice-cold in fact, and Dikha felt a tingling in her gut. 'Thank you,' Diksha said politely, taking the chance to get a closer look at her in the dim light of the stairway.

'Getting some air?' the woman asked Diksha, her voice throaty and full, the sound of wealth rippling in its undertones. Diksha nodded. This woman fascinated her. She had seemed to come from nowhere, no one seemed to know her, she looked nothing like everyone else around Diksha, with their uniform bodies and standard features.

'Hi, I'm Diksha.'

The woman smiled languorously, holding her hand out in a formal gesture for a handshake. Handshakes for introductions had gone out of use a couple of centuries ago when the Brotherhood had decided that bodily contact in public spaces was illegal. Her touch sent a buzz of chill through Diksha's spine.

'Pleased to meet you, Diksha,' she replied, 'Do you come here often?'

'Not very often, perhaps once or twice a month.'

'I've seen you around,' she said, her voice coming through the fronds of smoke she exhaled after a deep drag from the cigarette in her hand. 'Is that your boyfriend, the tall fellow you came in with? Do you have a pod booked for afterwards?'

'No, not my boyfriend. He's an asexual. So am I. He's here for the high of music. I don't...I've never been in a pod...'

Diksha had no idea why she was saying all of this to a stranger, this most uncool fact that she wasn't here for the one reason most came for – the pods, the nest of the forbidden that had survived all the cleansing attempts of the Brotherhood, that sprang up at different locations every month, moving to keep its regulars safe, were a place to allow the Pure to seek out the pleasure of touch, to keep humans from becoming the automatons the Brotherhood wanted them to be.

Diksha was different; she came here because she was curious. She didn't care about the hour in the pod with someone who was equally interested in you at no extra charge except for the entry charge. She had never felt the urge to touch or be touched, her body repulsed her when she looked at herself. Out of her overalls, she was long and lean, all angles and bones.

According to the Brotherhood, touch was a contaminant. Skin on skin was blasphemy now that they had decided who would be cloned and which genes were preferable. Everyone looked like they had the same parents. Light skinned, sharp-featured, tall, androgynous, created for efficiency in the rarified air under the Dome, created with the aesthetic the Committee had determined would be the ideal race to propagate for the Brotherhood. They were the chosen ones, the ones who would create the new nation, or populate new worlds, engineered to have the best brains and the golden looks of their long-dead ancestors. For generations of humans born not from the womb, the first experience of a mother's hug was the sterile touch of the CareCyborgs they were entrusted to for the first shaky months when they learnt how to navigate the world and take care of their bodies. There was no growing up because they emerged fully grown from the cocoons, their memories and identity imprinted by the Brotherhood, creating an assembly line of humans with ideal values and conveniently untarnished childhoods.

But where there was flesh, there was the need for touch, and desire survived in some subdued recess of their multicloned brains. As did the desire for pleasure, either through substance, music or other means, defying the Brotherhood who tried to control it. And so, the Pure rebelled against the ones who sought to control them. At least some of them did. Through acts that barely lasted for a few minutes but could doom them to the dungeons if they were caught. The dungeons were torture cells where they would be ripped organ by organ and fed to the infinite organ recycling centres for those living up on the surface.

Diksha had lived her life believing touch to be primitive. She believed she preferred mindfucks. Those who were swayed by touch were vulnerable to influence, to persuasion, to deception. Those weren't safe choices for the Inner Councils of the Brotherhood. She was ambitious, yes. Women weren't allowed into the Brotherhood. She would be the first.

But now, looking at this woman, she wasn't sure she cared anymore. She reached her hand out and caressed the woman's face. Her skin was alabaster smooth, gleaming gold in the faintness of the dim light trickling in from the closed pods that surrounded the dance floor. The woman pulled Diksha to her and put her cold arms around Diksha's trembling body. Her lips brushed against Diksha's, icy, and her tongue sought out Diksha's. She pushed Diksha against the wall, moving her hands over her body, cupping her butt, kneading her breasts, grinding her pubis against Diksha's. This was what the right touch did, Diksha realized. It dissolved you into waves of pleasure that wiped everything from your mind, except the need for more. When they broke apart, Diksha stared at her for a long moment and then took her hand. 'Let's find us a pod,' she said.

When she woke, she was curled up alone in the pod. Her clothes, which she had discarded in a flurry were folded and placed neatly on the shelf meant for clothes near the exit. The pod was still fragrant with the odour of bodily fluids, a scent Diksha hadn't known before. This is what it smelt liked – human desire.

She pulled on her clothes and pressed the button to open the pod. The discotheque was deserted, the other pods were open and empty of the copulating humans and cyborgs who had inhabited them through the night. By the glimmer of light sifting in through the slats on the boarded-up windows she knew it was day, and she had to find her way out without the drones seeing her.

She moved swiftly through the tentacled warren-like maze that led to the tenements opening onto the outside world. But the exit routes were now blocked. She was too late. The doors, reinforced steel, would not open without the password, which had now changed. She had been forgotten inside. Panic surged through her as she realized the air supply would be turned off soon. Within an hour, her lungs would use up the emergency stash of air in the canister in her body suit. She would die. She sat down on the dank floor of the corridor, her brain blank and her heart racing painfully against her chest.

*I am going to die here,* she thought. *And I will never make it to the Council.* If what had happened here was ever released to the Brotherhood, she would be relegated to a Worker, condemned to shovel, carry, clean, paint, repair and maintain the essentials under this gigantic Dome.

After several minutes, which felt to her like hours, the first rush of panic and anxiety passed, and the instinct for survival took over. After all, the core of her that was reptilian had survived erasure even though she had been cloned and mutated some 20 times over to reach the zenith of the ideal brain and body perfection that the Aesthetic Human Resources department established by the Brotherhood strived for.

She needed to find her way out of the maze, perhaps back through the main door, the one that was boarded up, the one with the two gigantic statues next to it. A door they never used because it opened on to the road and exposed them to the all-seeing drones. Once upon a time it had been a bank, when humans had traded with something they called money. It had been the most powerful bank in the country and controlled all its economic activity. Now the currency they used was cryptocash stored in skin wallets that they could access only by retinal unlocking on their handscreens. Currency was irrelevant in her world, where wealth was thought and leisure was work, and no one came here anymore, except those who knew what the place morphed into on certain nights of the month.

The sun was climbing higher, it was getting warmer inside the shelled-out edifice. Knowing she had to hurry, she ran past the detritus of the previous night's shenanigans. Dust motes swarmed up and scattered with every footstep she took. An occasional pigeon fluttered around, confused at being disturbed at this time of the day. Were there eyes here, hidden in the ceiling, embedded in the stone, that were watching her scramble around trying to find an escape route? When it came into view, the door was slightly ajar. It seemed so easy to step out and hail a passing flycab. The world outside beckoned her.

She approached the door cautiously, feeling soft gusts of wind move through her hair at once like a caress and a threat. The door was kept partially open, she realized, by the foot of a person lying at the step. She breathed in sharply as she bent forward to take a closer look. It was the man who had been dancing with the unknown woman she'd spent the previous night with. They had disappeared while dancing, she remembered, for that short moment when the light went out and she hadn't seen him again all night. And here he was, lying with his skin a deathly blue from the cold, his eyes open and unseeing, and his chest unmoving.

Diksha slipped out of the door, stepping carefully over the corpse. The morning was a cold one, the sun was a faint round blob beyond the pall of poisonous haze above the Dome. She wondered if she should call the PeaceKeepers and inform them about the dead man. They would find him themselves, she decided; she had best get out of there and back to her cell. She rushed down the crumbling stone stairs towards the huge gates down the driveway, preparing herself to climb over them if needed, but stumbled as she felt the tiny hair at the nape of her neck prickle. A human instinct, residual, despite the relentless efforts to eradicate unwanted instinctive responses.

Someone was watching her.

She steadied herself on the last step but one and turned around. There was no one there, only the stone statue of the ancient *yakshi* standing sentinel over the ruins of what had once been a revered institution, her gaze impassive, blank, unseeing.

# THE GATEKEEPER'S INTERN

## RUCHIKA ROY

*It's all about energy.*

In the darkness that engulfed me while the doctors tried to revive my heart, these were the words that I had heard. It had felt like I was wading through a gluey, black miasma, but through it all, it was her distinctive golden-edged voice that had pulled me forward. She was speaking of the energy of atoms. According to Moira, it was also the energy of magic.

Ten minutes and 37 seconds.

That's how long I'd been clinically dead after my car was struck by a freak bolt of lightning. My parents, who were there with me, didn't make it. Their hearts stopped permanently when approximately one billion joules of energy ripped through them as we were driving back from their laboratory. The car acted as a grotesque conductor, frying everything that had contact with it. After a few days in a coma, when I woke up, they told me that I had suffered burns down my throat — as if I'd lost a screaming match with nature.

I couldn't speak for days. But this suited me just fine. It wasn't like I had a lot to say about being dead. There had been no blinding flash of warm, inviting light. No long-dead grandparents waiting for me on the 'other side'. There was no other side, really. All I could remember was utter blackness, like a night spent deep underwater with no hope or expectation of dawn.

In fact, the only thing I really remembered about that night was from before the accident. My parents and I had walked out of their laboratory. They had been arguing about their work — something about clean energy and its uses in defence technology. I didn't pay attention to what they were saying, and all I could think about later was that if I hadn't shown up there unannounced, they would not have had to bring me back home through a massive thunderstorm. If I hadn't been there, they would have argued but within the safe confines of their office. If I hadn't been there, they would have still been alive.

But there I was, back at college after three months, and this is what I knew — my parents were dead, there was no afterlife and I had no plans for my future. After all, did it matter what you did if the only people you wanted to impress had left you forever without so much as a goodbye? I didn't think so. Instead, my plan was to find an unobtrusive corner where I could count out the interminable seconds and hope life passed me by without any additional drama.

I woke up with a start. The auditorium I normally escaped to for its silence was filling up with people. I looked around and saw their listless faces as they prepared for one more pointless career-counselling symposium. I got up to leave and had almost reached the door, when a soft gasp escaped the crowd. I turned to look – and there she was. Walking on to the stage, somehow tall despite being only five foot and some change, wearing a simple muslin saree in a shocking shade of purple, adorned with no jewellery except a wide silver cuff on her wrist, Moira was a vision. Quite simply, she was beautiful, and when she looked straight into my eyes, I sat back down on the nearest seat.

*If you can hear me, you shouldn't worry.*

Even though her lips had not moved, I knew, without a doubt, that it was her voice in my head. I would have known that gold-edged voice anywhere. The nearest person was two rows away, sitting by himself, staring intently at her but she was looking directly at me. Even as Professor Sainik, the guidance counsellor and resident shrink, introduced her and told us what she was going to talk about, Moira didn't take her eyes off me.

*Yes, it's me. Moira. Don't be alarmed.*

'What the hell…'

Unlike her, I'd spoken out loud. The boy sitting two rows away turned to look at me irritably. I recognized him as the secretary of the Extracurricular Society and most likely the person responsible for organizing this event. When I looked back on to the stage, I saw Moira gracefully carry her papers to the podium.

*Do you remember me at all? You're probably wondering why this is happening. It's really quite simple – you said you would return, and I'm here to take you back where you belong.*

'Good morning. Today, I want to discuss a fairly basic idea with you all – what is your purpose?' On stage, Moira had started her prepared speech, but the voice in my head continued regardless.

*Don't you have questions about why you're alive today?*

'All of us, from when we are young, have ambitions. It starts with something as simple as dreams of "When I grow up", and goes on to ,"When I graduate", and continues to "When I have enough money", and so on.'

*Do you know why you survived that lightning storm? Do you know where your parents are?*

This was it, I thought in panic. This was what it felt like to finally lose your mind. The voices in my head had woken up and I was simply too dumb to realize what the rest of the world already knew – I was done for.

*If you want to know more, meet me where the lightning struck and maybe you'll believe me.*

I got up abruptly from my seat. Despite the creaking and shuffling that accompanied my hurried exit, the boy in front didn't look back at me even once. Nor did Moira. In fact, nobody moved. Nobody even blinked. I looked at Professor Sainik and saw that the pen that had slipped from her grip was suspended in mid-air, her embarrassed expression frozen in time.

*Don't be late. We don't have much time.*

I ran out of the auditorium, unnoticed, and dashed through the open grounds of the college, past a tableau of my classmates frozen mid-action, a noiseless scream ripping from my throat. It's a trick, it's only a trick – I'm not going crazy, I told myself.

*It's all about energy.* The words dropped into my head again, sending ripples through every part of my body.

\*\*\*

Many hours later, I found myself at the same spot I'd last seen my parents alive. It was a scorched tree that was split down the middle, destined for the lumberyard whenever the municipal authorities got to it. It was here I found myself face-to-face with Moira. This time, dressed in a cobalt blue velvet overcoat thrown casually over ripped boyfriend jeans, she looked exactly like what she was – a person straddling two worlds, belonging to neither. As I stood opposite her, wondering where the intervening hours had gone, Moira just leaned back against the tree and looked around, like a tourist. 'You know, they didn't tell me it was going to be you in that auditorium. All I knew is that I had to collect a Bridger and bring her – or him – back,' she said.

'Bridger?'

'Yes, that's you. You crossed over and then crossed back. Both the gates were open to you, and that is really rare. I explained all this to you already the last time you made the trip. Don't you remember?'

'Made the trip?'

'When you died, sweety.' She smiled at me with what must have been kindness, but all I felt was a cold ball of dread spreading its tentacles across my gut.

My utter incomprehension must have been apparent because something dimmed in her eyes. Then she pulled out a notebook and started to draw.

'Okay, a quick recap then. Think of the world as two circles that intersect. One circle is Reality, the real world of college and friends and jobs and bills. The other is the different one – the 'Unknown'. The Unknown houses the gods and the future, the imaginary and the impossible. And in between Reality and the Unknown, there lies the Bridge.'

'Only the dead – or those considered insane – are able to perceive both these worlds. But, even then, most of them can only travel from one to the other and *never* travel back. But every few years or centuries there is someone who goes across and makes it back. Like you. And we call them Bridgers.'

As I heard her speak, I relaxed. She was mistaken. I had been dead, and all I had perceived was a whole lot of nothing. As much as I wanted to believe that all of this life, pain and loss meant something, that there was more out there, Moira was clearly just a strangely dressed woman with a few tricks up her sleeve. She was wrong, there was no big plan, and for just a moment, I felt regret.

*I'm not wrong. You just don't remember. Those 10 minutes and 37 seconds were very different in our world. In the Unknown, we can make time collapse or expand depending on our needs. And in those minutes or months, you and I met and fell in love. You wanted to stay but somehow you also felt the pull to return. And on your last day there, you promised you would come back. But you never did. I guess that's why they sent me where they did in search of a Bridger.*

She smiled at me as she spoke inside my head. Just as I was about to argue, she leaned forward and kissed me.

I was a 19-year-old heartbroken orphan and I'd never been kissed by a girl; not that I could remember. But when Moira kissed me, the softest touch of her lips on mine, I was transported to a time without tears.

A long time ago, my mother had told me what her first real kiss was like. She had said that it felt like she was home. And it wasn't with my father. Kissing Moira felt like I was breathing her in, letting her into the atoms that made up my body, and letting myself settle into hers. It was the kind of kiss that lasted your whole life. And it was unexpected. That's when I felt it — the magic that nestled in her bones. It was new yet ancient; it was wild yet completely controlled. It spanned millennia and was yet contained in the moment.

As she leaned back, I tried to claw my way back to reality. It's a trick. It's a game. It's not real, my mind raced. Aloud I said, 'We were…in love?'

She smiled. Before she could answer, I heard the crunch of gravel behind us. 'Are we done here?' a bored voice drawled. I turned around and saw him — the same secretary of the Extracurricular Society, wearing a leather jacket and a bad attitude. Something told me that he was much more than a loiterer in college halls, and maybe if I looked closer, I'd see the many worlds that he was straddling as well. Looking only at Moira he said, 'We need to get to the ferry.'

'Yes, Sameer, I just need a minute,' she said. Moira took my hand and pulled me to my feet, at once stepping closer to me. Standing close to me, she was small, but formidable. 'If you come with us, everything you know will change. You will find the answers you seek, but you will also find questions that will stretch the very boundaries of your reality. But this is your choice and you have to make it *now*.'

It was night. Again, hours had passed, but I didn't remember. It was as if my mind had created a darkness within it to block out parts of my life that were possibly too scary to contemplate. I was standing on the edge of the narrow inlet that came in from the Arabian Sea. It was really dark, and an unlikely mist covered the ground. I could hear the sound of water lapping close by. There were no lights; dawn seemed forever away. Moira stood next to me, looking out towards the pitch-black of the flowing creek. She glanced at me briefly. 'You lost time again, right?' I nodded mutely, shaken but also strangely calm. Maybe that's what happens when you return from the dead, I told myself. 'Don't worry, you will remember everything when you're not afraid anymore.' She smiled and looked back towards the creek. Maybe she was right. Maybe there was nothing to fear —

Except the Unknown.

I looked around. 'Isn't this...' I recognized the place.

'We are at the regular jetty,' Moira said. 'But we have a different ride.' She glanced at me and then stepped forward. Out of the inky surroundings, a tiny iridescent sailboat emerged. The sails billowed out in the strange, windless surroundings, pulling the boat closer to shore. As it approached, I saw the formless mist pull itself off the ground, like a gentle fountain, and take the shape of human beings. Somewhere in the distance, a clock struck 4 a.m. 'The darkest hour', my literature professor used to say.

Moira watched me look at the people of the mist. Everyone seemed to be waiting for the same boat. They look like ghosts, I thought to myself.

Moira answered, 'I suppose you could say that. But "ghosts" are really the energy of the dead.' My confusion deepened, I turned to her, frowning. She continued, as if explaining something obvious. 'Everything is energy. People, oceans, trees, insects – they're all energy. It's energy that makes the blood pump through your arteries, it's energy that helps bees fly, it's energy that makes waves crest in the oceans. And since energy can only be transformed, when people die it's their residual energy that we harness. You will have heard such words as 'spirits' or 'poltergeists', but it's just positive or negative energy. Like protons or electrons. And, like in the atom, which has a neutron to balance it all, in the great Unknown we are the Balancers.'

So this was the energy of atoms. And of magic.

Before I could say anything more, the boat docked, and the dead floated on board. Moira and I followed. I saw Sameer at the ropes, the muscles in his arms corded as he grappled to get the sails to do his bidding. In my head, unbidden, flashed a memory of those arms holding me. Moira saw me watching him and something sparked in her eyes. She said, 'He's the Traveller.

He travels through reality, using time and its elements to get to where he is needed at any point. Haven't you noticed how he is always around? He helps us out whenever we need him.'

'And did he also...'

'Die? Yes. See that scar over his right eyebrow? That was the incision that was made to lobotomize him. His blood pressure spiked and he flatlined on the table. They didn't know then as much as they do today, but I guess witches with visions were being tortured and killed for a lot less in those days.'

'Those days...?'

'Sameer was born in 1487 and died in 1512 in a royal surgeon's experiment room during the rule of the talented but limited Sultan of Delhi. Today, in your Reality, he is more than five hundred years old. Relatively young in our line of work.'

As I looked at him in surprise, I could have sworn he smirked at me. I looked away. Yes, Moira had kissed me, and maybe I'd loved her in the Unknown, but it was the ancient and beautiful Sameer who was making me uncomfortable in a very real way. He was not a stranger, of that I was certain. Moira grinned at me and I rushed to change the subject. 'Why is it a ferry? Why not something else?'

Moira looked at me and suddenly it seemed as if the millennia were catching up with her.

'It's because water is the best conductor of energy. Haven't you ever wondered why the earth and human beings are both about 80 per cent water? It's through water that we transmit power to each other – and not just power. Ideas, messages, sometimes entire blueprints of concepts. That's how sometimes you'll see the same story ideas or even inventions originating simultaneously in different parts of the world. Most people call it a "gut feeling" but it is just the water in your body communicating with us.'

'Who is "us"?'

Moira grinned. 'We call ourselves the Department of Originals and Replacements, or the DOORS. A few decades ago, a musician died of an overdose but was revived. In that time, he saw us, found out what we did, but chose to go a different way. He forgot everything when he returned, but something must have stuck because I believe he started a band in our name?' I nodded, amused, and Moira shrugged. 'The real DOORS, however, is a real place with, needless to say, actual doors but these doors have been designed to allow in only a very specific kind of person – the dead kind. Like most places with entry restrictions, there is a Gatekeeper at the entrance and these days, that's me.'

'Wait a second, are you a god of some kind?'

'Oh no! That's way above my pay grade. I'm just an Original.' Then, sensing my next question, she continued, 'About fifty thousand years ago, the Originals were creatures made of the elements. You had earth, air, water, fire and time. Combine all of these, and you created an entity. This entity could travel the planet and transform itself into any shape or form, even into the figurative "spark" in the human mind. It was this spark that led to cave paintings, inventions, songs, books, innovations and crazy advancements, all of which have made one of Earth's weakest species, its most dominant. The real gods used to believe that human beings had the capacity to evolve into magical beings and the gods created the Originals to help them.'

'Used to believe? You mean they don't anymore?'

Moira sighed and looked off into the darkness. The silence was only broken by the soft sounds of the water lapping against the sides of the boat. I looked at Sameer, who merely shrugged. Just as I was about to repeat myself, Moira turned to me, in her eyes a deep sadness I had not seen before. 'I don't know what they believe anymore. I mean, with seven billion human souls capable of magic, one would think Reality would be a lot better, right? But, instead, you guys are just slowly but surely tearing each other and the planet apart while simultaneously calling on the Unkonwn for help to fix the messes. But the truth is, we can't keep up the repairs!'

Moira stood up and walked away, towards the front of the boat. As I watched her standing alone, staring at unseen things, I felt Sameer sit down next to me. 'It's not their fault really. As the human population kept growing, the Originals needed help to keep up. That's when they started using the soul energy of the dead to help out, to carry messages. But the more soul energies they harnessed, the more volatile the system became, and the more they needed people like us — the Bridgers, the Balancers. And those are few and far between.'

I turned back to look at where Moira was standing, only to find her intense stare on me. Then her voice filled my mind.

*The truth is there aren't enough Balancers for the number of souls we have. But if the energies discover that we're outnumbered, we will have a war on our hands — a war with catastrophic consequences on Reality and the Unknown. That's part of the reason you need to be here. But you have to choose to belong, to choose this life, to be my replacement when the time is right… But, before all that, there's a lot more you need to know.*

Moira's thought inside my head was interrupted by the shuddering of the boat on gravel as it docked. The soul energies floated off and melted into the queue that had formed ahead. Moira leapt off the side and rushed forward to what looked like an innocuous gate, almost crumbling in parts.

'Welcome to the Unknown,' Moira said, as she jogged ahead.

I looked back to see Sameer already preparing for his journey back. 'You're not coming?' I said, surprised.

He shrugged and replied, 'I'm a Traveller, princess, and there are many more trips I have to plan around the world. But if you ever need a ride, just call me.' And, with that, he set off across the creek.

*Just call? How?*

I didn't have time to question him as I was pulled along with the souls to the entrance. As I crossed it, I was covered by a light mist of water. Almost immediately, I felt ligher, as if the weight of Reality had been stripped away. I couldn't understand why I'd almost chosen to not return. When I wiped the spray out of my eyes, I was taken aback by what I saw before me. What had arguably been an extremely underwhelming entrance gate to the Unknown was now transformed into a gorgeous edifice made entirely of crystal, the night-time gloom had changed to an effervescent golden light, and even the soul energies seemed more solid, more real. They had started changing colour as they walked through the light mist.

'It's the true colour of their energy. Reds and Oranges have a positive charge, Blues and Greens have a negative one,' Moira said. I saw her standing behind the counter. She had earlier been dressed in velvet and denims, but now she was covered in dull gold, the surrounding light glinting off her clothes in a way that reminded me of sunsets. As each soul drifted past her desk, a gilt-edged sheet of vintage paper appeared in front of her. As she read it, it automatically got filled in with all the details of the people walking in. Moira quickly glanced through each document and pushed them through a pigeonhole. Each soul would go through the gate and step on a black metal plate on wheels made of light. As Moira classified their history, the black plates would whisk them away somewhere.

As I watched Moira work, a woman about my age materialized next to me. Her body was a shade of blue and she was dressed in white. As I looked closer, she appeared a bit blurred around the edges.

'Hi! I'm Kaveri, I'm a soul energy,' she said.

'Uh, hi… I'm…'

'Oh, I know who you are! You're the possible new recruit but *shh*! No one can know, okay? Moira insisted on it.' I grinned as she took my hand and led me behind the counter. 'I'm supposed to take you around and show you things. I was supposed to be assigned a few months ago but Moira needed help. So, I decided to stay back, be her temporary Intern, learn what's what.'

I laughed. 'And what is what?'

'It's very exciting. See, I'm a Blue, which is just an official way of saying 'someone with negative charge.'' As Kaveri explained the details, she began to lead me away from Moira and the bustle of activity at the Gate of the Unknown, through what seemed like the administrative wing of the place. It looked like a gigantic unending library with row upon row of burnished file cabinets that were automatically collecting the gilt-edged documents that Moira was categorizing. The files were in different shades of the colour spectrum. Kaveri continued. 'I turned Blue thanks to Reality problems – childhood trauma, abuse, bad experiences or whatever, until finally I just became depressed, angry and cynical. So, when I died – I was murdered, you know – my soul charge was negative, blue.'

She pulled out an orange file and opened it. Inside was a photograph of a middle-aged man with his Reality details written out. Kaveri smiled. 'Now this guy – we call them Reals, these people in Reality – he had supportive parents, did okay in school. But he was also poor and had health and financial problems too. However, despite all that, he basically always looked on the bright side of things. When he died, he became a positive charge. That's why he's an Orange,' she said as she flipped a page. 'But look at this...' She pulled out another sheet from his folder and handed it to me. It was titled *Intervention*. 'You see this? The blue markings?' Kaveri pointed out dates and events. 'Blue markings mean a significant negative charge was added to his life...' I was confused but she turned another page and then stopped at a paragraph. 'Ah, here it is. See? When he was 15 years old, this guy had recurring nightmares of not being able to walk. That fear prompted him to take up sports seriously, and then he started his own gymnasium where he taught self-defence to young girls. Now that's a negative charge like me being used as a recurring nightmare to generate fear, but ultimately resulting in a positive change in Reality. Get it?'

I wasn't sure I did, but her enthusiasm was infectious, so I nodded. She continued, 'I can't wait to be assigned. There are so many departments here and even if I'm not formally invited into Nightmares, I'll be happy to even work in the Department of Visions and Miracles, or Ideas and Inspiration. I'll take anything at all, so long as they let me do really messed up things.'

'Messed up, in what way?'

'Oh! Like, in Visions, an Orange could probably make water seem like wine for the Reals while I, as a Blue, can make them see rivers of blood or ferocious lightning...'

Kaveri stopped, her hand on her mouth. 'I'm so sorry...the lightning...your parents...'

I shrugged. 'It's okay...'

Quite suddenly, an alarm rang through the area. The golden light was covered by an angry, sparking darkness. Sirens erupted from different corners of the Unknown and everyone looked around, scared. Kaveri tried to pull me to a corner, but I ran out, looking for Moira. A wind had kicked up, lifting the gilt-edged documents out of their assigned files into a frenzied sparkling tornado. At the far edges of the dark mass, I saw a sight that terrified me — it was as if the very molecules of air were starting to glow, becoming hotter by the second. And as the edges sparked and grew, I suddenly remembered.

My parents had been in the front seat of the battered car, still arguing about their project that revolved around nuclear fusion. My father wanted to simply follow the science regardless of consequences, and my mother was terrified of what the people who would ultimately get to wield this power would be able to do. I had sat, ignored, in the back seat, hoping for something that would make them notice me.

As the memory played out in my mind, I wondered if somewhere, I'd wished for what happened next. That afternoon, I had looked out of the window to see big droplets of rain start to spatter across the windshield and, immersed as they were in their ideological differences, neither of my parents noticed that the ground had begun to shift. Before I could utter a word, my father lost control of the car, and drove it off the road, smashing into a large banyan tree. The impact threw me out of the back seat, on to the ground a few feet away, my head smashing against a rock. Dazed, I looked at my parents who were struggling to get out. It had become very quiet and I had seen the glowing molecules of air dancing in the air around me. They were getting super-heated and were turning brighter with every passing second. Then they all seemed to coalesce in a blinding flash of light. I remember a scream renting the air, remember recognizing it as mine. The last thing I recall are my mother's tearful eyes, staring at me through the shattered window, her lips forming soundless words as a sharp shard of light hit the tree, then the car and, finally, me.

I snapped back to the present, shaken by what I had remembered. I looked around the Unknown, at the scattering soul energies and gold-clad Originals and their Interns racing for safety. I spun around, trying to spot Moira and I remembered something else – I remembered running back home from college the day I'd seen Moira in the auditorium. The house was empty, and I'd run to my room. Sameer had been sitting on my bed looking like he belonged there. He looked at my terrified face and said, 'This is your life now, princess. Enough of running away from guilt. You can choose to ignore it, or you can choose to do something about it. But sooner or later, you will remember everything and it will hurt like crazy. One thing you can't do however is go back to not knowing.' I had burst into tears then, for the first time since I'd woken up from being dead. I thought of my parents, of everything I had lost, of being more alone than I had ever imagined. And Sameer had held me until I'd stopped. He said, 'I took your parents to the other side. Don't you want to see them one more time?' And that's when I'd gone to see Moira at the tree, where she had kissed me.

Back in the present, high above the crystal roof of the Unknown, I could see that the darkness was in truth a reddish-orange haze surrounded by blue-grey lightning clouds. And all of it seemed to be concentrating in a downward spiral in the distance. Kaveri materialized next to me, looking aghast. She said, 'It's a Charge battle. There aren't enough Balancers in the Unknown, so negative and positive charges spill over and fight for supremacy. Any side that wins gets to decide what kind of feelings the people in Reality will experience.'

'What will happen then?' I shouted to be heard above the loud snapping of the energy molecules as they circled above us. Kaveri shook her head. 'I don't know... If the negative charges win, people in Reality could suffer massive bouts of depression, they could just decide to bomb each other because an all-pervasive sense of hopelessness will descend on them. If the positive charges win, the levels of euphoria in people will increase — something like what a shot of heroin feels like. They would stop doing things. Parents would abandon children, people would stop going to work, infrastructure would fall apart... Without balance, this could be catastrophic for Reality.'

So this is what Moira had meant. As I looked around me, at the angry, swirling blue and orange hues of soul energies, I realized that this was what Balancers did — control this crazy force that could otherwise be unleashed on Reality and affect the real feelings of real people. How could Moira have possibly thought that I, who could barely even control my tears, do this?

I have to find Moira, I thought frantically, as the winds whipped around me. I had to tell her that she had the wrong person, before it was too late. Just then, in the distance, I saw her in her flowing gold jacket, dive into the middle of the Charge battle. I raced after her, unheeding of the shouting around me. As I got closer to the battle, I could feel the static in the air start to cling to me. The molecules of air got brighter the closer I got. Finally, I turned a corner and saw, in the middle of an open field, not two clouds, but two armies of soul energies facing each other with Moira in the middle.

I started running toward her when I heard her.

*Wait! Stop! Don't come closer!*

'Moira?'

*There's so much I have to tell you but I'm not going to have the time.*

I can't do this Moira! It's too much!

*Yes, you can. You already have it in you. You have survived anger, loss, loneliness, even death, and you're still here, looking for something to believe in. You still have hope and that is everything! The fate of the world rests on people like you. Because you can take all the negativity in the world and change it to something magical. But you have to choose this life. What do you choose?*

I looked at the energies around her. I saw her straining with the effort to control them. But, despite what it must have been costing her, she waited for me to answer. And at that moment, I saw them. My parents had materialized among the soul energies, and they were looking directly at me. Surrounded by all the lightning and electricity, it felt like I was on the verge of losing them all over again.

Moira saw them too, and turned to me. *You will be able to finally help them, and many others like them, if you agree.*

I tasted the salt of the tears that must have been streaming down my face. *I'll do it Moira but I don't know how!*

She smiled. *You already know how to use your thoughts. The rest, you'll learn. Because you are henceforth the Gatekeeper's Intern.*

It happened in a flash of light, but it felt like hours. Moira looked peaceful as she communicated with me. Her hair was spread out around her face, the electric charge making her muscles rigid. I looked towards the energies as they swirled around her. Then Moira smiled at me, looked up and screamed. Light burst out of her and scattered into a million tiny beads of iridescent brightness that shaped themselves to form an impermeable dome around the field. And within that dome, I saw the angered soul energies charge towards Moira and then, everything exploded, contained only by the light that Moira had released.

As quickly as it had begun, it was over. The field was empty, only the smell of burning metal lingered in the air. And Moira was gone, just like my parents. The sunlight returned to drench the surroundings again, but I couldn't look around. I could feel a loss so deep within me that I had no place left for anything like beauty.

I walked back to the boat that had just docked and Sameer leaned out. 'You thought of me, princess?' We looked at each other for a long moment and then I said, 'She's gone.'

Sameer looked stricken for a moment but then he smiled. 'Moira is an Original, made of the energy of the elements. And energy is never gone, only transformed. Or weren't you paying attention in science class?'

I looked at his twisted smile, and for the first time in a very long while I allowed myself to recognize hope.

'Are you staying or returning to Reality?' he asked me.

I shrugged, looking back at the world that I had just been shown. The Unknown had my parents and Moira in it. In just a few moments, I had found a foothold in a place which had people I cared about. But, as Moira had said, it was Reality that needed saving and, for that, the Unknown needed more Bridgers like me.

'I need to go back. But things have to be different. I need to be different, I need to know more…' I said to Sameer. He smiled and gestured me on board. 'Moira nominated you her Intern. Which basically means that as far as Reality or the Unknown is concerned, you are the interim Gatekeeper. And that means you can bend time as much as you need. So take as long as you want to study up. You now have the power of the Unknown with you and, with a little practice, you can do anything and be whoever you choose for as long as it pleases you. And I will help you.'

I smiled and got on board. As the boat moved away from the shore, I looked back at Kaveri, who waved at me before she went back to sorting out the gilt-edged documents in front of her. I sat down next to Sameer and looked towards the setting sun as I began to wonder if I could possibly live up to Moira's expectations.

***

Many years passed as I journeyed through the Unknown, learning to bend time and the elements of the land. I thought of Moira often, especially about the day I first saw her in that auditorium. I still didn't remember everything about those 10 minutes and 37 seconds but the more time I spent doing her job, the more I understood her and how lonely her job had been. Today, in Reality, only three months after I had first learned of the Unknown, she was suddenly on my mind again. Maybe it had something to do with where I found myself – a college auditorium.

A voice broke into my thoughts. 'And now, it's my pleasure to introduce you to our speaker of the day, Ms…,' the professor suddenly looked confused, as if she couldn't remember my name. She turned to me with an embarrassed smile and I stepped out from the darkened confines of the wings on to a brightly-lit stage. As I stepped towards the podium, I heard a soft gasp escape from the audience just as the professor shuffled through her cue-cards looking for a name. And then I smiled and stopped time.

*'If you can hear me, you needn't worry. You're not going crazy.'* I looked around the faceless sea of people around me.

'Did she just say something?' I heard a voice mutter in the darkness.

I smiled as I locked eyes with him. *It's all about energy*, I said gently.

# GRANDMA GARAM'S KITTY PARTY

## SHWETA TANEJA

The crackle of lightning split the moonless sky, unsuccessfully trying to burn it. Owls hooted in alarm. Mangroves slithered snake-like as the wind sang ominously through them. Jaanu frowned, looking up at the cloud-laden sky, heavy with the promise of monsoon. It was the perfect setting for a kitty party, and she would hate to ruin it. But she just *had* to do it tonight.

She wrung her white saree's pallu, slapping it onto her shoulder. Pursing her full black lips, she strode deeper into the island, stopping abruptly as she felt a tug somewhere deep in the pit of her stomach.

'By grandma's burnt cat,' she cursed under her breath, warily eyeing the direction from which the call had come. 'Not tonight, please.'

'Jaaanooo… Jaanujaanujaaaaaaaanu… Come to me, Jaanu…'

'I've had it with being a chudail!' she stomped her foot angrily, as a barb twisted in her stomach.

'Jaaanu…'

'Fine, fine,' she hissed in the direction of the voice, her stomach now a melted candle.

The wheedling voice came attached to the power of a captive spell that no chudail could resist. Involuntarily, she followed the trails of the voice, gliding to the far end of the island until she reached a clump of bushes that threw long shadows around a small mound of rocks. A middle-aged man was crouched on one of the rocks, naked, his stomach jiggling precariously, stoking a fire in a makeshift depression. He methodically fed it clumps of hair as he continued to call out her name in a nasal tone. Jaanu touched her newly styled bob. So that's where that wretched barber had disposed of her hair. No wonder the call had been so powerful.

'Jaaaaanooo…'

'Yes, I'm here,' she barked, solidifying so that she could be seen. 'What do you want?'

The man started and tumbled backwards, splatting his hand into the fire he'd made, its heat making him jump and scream. Jaanu took a deep breath. Not even a professional. It had to be a comical amateur crashing a kitty party, of all things, the annual event hosted by her grandma, where all of her predatory sisters gathered to sacrifice cats as an offering to Ma Chudail, the mother of all chudails. The goddess of irony definitely liked her toes tickled.

The man tumbled, wheeled around and straightened, still shivering like a leaf in a storm, his eyes double the size of his shrunken balls as he ogled her knees.

'You stupid man!' she rasped. 'Leave, you're in danger here!'

'Please don't eat me,' he yowled, crossing his arms to protect his groin.

Jaanu groaned. 'I'm vegan,' she said matter-of-factly.

He didn't seem to hear her as he fished desperately in his bag, his eyes glued on her. He pulled out a crumpled piece of paper, opening it and squinting to read from it. '*Manshun jabaar chudail naale…*'

'That wouldn't work on any chudail,' Jaanu sighed.

'…*baa araa*…' He stopped, frowning, looking rapidly from the paper to her and back. 'But…but I paid fifty thousand rupees for this *junglee* chudail *totka*!'

'Heard of internet scams before?' she said, stepping towards him. 'And now you need to leave!'

'P-p-lease don't hurt me! I'm innocent. All I wanted to do is… to see your feet. I've never seen real chudail feet. Please. *Once.*'

'My feet?'

'I know it's not normal, but…'

*Normal.* The word hammered at her heart. So, she was not so very different from this silly little creature. Both of them wanted things that weren't 'normal' for them. She glided up to him, crouched by his side, as he shrank back, terror in his eyes.

'Will you leave if I show you my feet?' she whispered.

He gulped and nodded, a nervous smile now wavering on his lips.

She pulled her white saree upto her knees. Her large black bark-like feet glistened in the dark night, pointing backwards, the nails on her knobbly toes overgrown with fungus. The man's Adam's apple bobbed as he inched his hand towards her foot.

'What the hell are you doing?' she snapped.

'Can I…' He gulped and wiped his fingers on his thinning hair, 'please let me…touch…*massage* your feet.'

'*What?*' Jaanu hollered furiously, pulling her feet away and standing up.

'You called me so you could massage my feet? Are you crazy? It's the night of Grandma's kitty party. Be thankful I was the one who answered your call and not one of the oth…'

'Our little black moon!'

Jaanu whipped around. Shit. Her cousins, the twins Muffin and Sweety loped into the glade, claws on sexy waists, dressed in white sarees like hers, their long black hair curling like snakes around their shapely bodies, faces wan with dramatically kohled eyes and red lips.

'She decided to come!' cried Sweety, grinning to show her perfectly polished fangs.

'And she brought a delicious gift.'

'He's not…' began Jaanu, but the twins leaped in her direction and roughly tumbled into her, making her stagger at the assault by their collective weight.

'Here, here, give me a bite!' said Sweety. 'I've missed you.'

'We were drinking together at the Bachhalan bar just last week, Sweety,' Jaanu said, dutifully biting her cousin's cheek. 'You girls are so dramatic!'

Muffin turned to the man. Her eyes pinpointed. 'Aren't you the Fetish Man?' she asked sharply.

'Fetish Man?' said Jaanu.

'He's the one who keeps summoning chudails from all over the city just so he can tickle their feet,' giggled Sweety. 'He did mine with a feather. It was kind of *o-kay*.'

'Ugh,' said Muffin, 'I hate anyone touching my barks.'

'It was just boring, you know?' said Sweety.

'He told me this was his first time!' said Jaanu.

'Oh, no, no,' said Muffin, 'Fetish Man loves to play the virgin card. Did he also say he can't help himself? He calls a new chudail every *Amavasya*. How many chudail feet have you touched, Fetish Man?'

'Actually…' said Fetish Man, wiping the sweat off his head and looking at Jaanu with a creepy puppy face, 'you're my first *junglee* chudail.'

'*Junglee*? Our Jaanu? She is a college graduate in philo-philo, Mister Fetish!' Sweety screeched. Muffin placed a strategic claw under his chin, making him gulp furiously.

'But – but her name's doing the rounds on our WhatsThat group…' he said plaintively.

'What's *what* group?' cried Jaanu.

'For people who like…umm…special feet,' he said, staring at Jaanu's ankles.

'Aww, this one's too much! We will give you a special night, Fetish Man,' purred Muffin. 'We were looking for a kitty to play with.' She licked his flabby cheek. The man shivered.

'Is she scaring you, you poor thing?' said Sweety. 'Don't worry, I'll take care of all your needs.' She moved her claw up the man's groin.

'Aaaarrgh!' he howled, and promptly fainted.

Sweety and Muffin cackled in unison as they picked the man off the ground and held him like a sack, one grabbing his arms, the other his legs.

'Come, Jaanu!' said Muffin, 'I'm thirsty for some catrum.'

Jaanu glumly followed her sisters to the centre of the marshland. She shouldn't have come. It already looked like she'd made a huge, huge mistake.

'I'm glad you came, Jaanu!' Sweety said, glancing back. 'Yeah, you had us scared last week with your hair cut and your thoughts on joining that useless cult,' said Muffin, deliberately dangling her arms so the Fetish Man's head banged against a rock.

'Straighteners are not a cult but a belief system,' said Jaanu. 'I think chudailism is barbaric and needs to be reinvigorated with fresh ideas to fit into modern mainstream society – '

'So you're going to do it?' asked Sweety.

'Yes, I'm determined to. I want a civilized life.' Jaanu pointed at the unconscious man who was flip-flopping like a hammock between their arms, 'Not this...madness.'

The metallic waft of burning flesh and blood announced the kitty party before they saw anyone. The tangle of mangroves cleared to reveal a feast in full swing, with chudails dancing, hollering, yapping, cackling and grabbing each other in fierce embraces. Muffin and Sweety unceremoniously dumped the still-unconscious Fetish Man. In unison, they glided towards the centre of the glade, calling on a gust that spiralled around them, making their hair gleam serpentine and their chiffon sarees move in swirls. The party sunk into a fascinated silence. Jaanu stared too, mouth agape. Though she'd seen her cousins' Bollywood performance on screen and in life so many times, she was, as always, fascinated by the two girls. They were naturals at being chudails – complete with an alien sexiness and husky voices, and the right amount of unethical cruelty to pursue horny men and their rasa. Unlike Jaanu, who had always struggled with her legacy.

The glade resounded with thunderous claps and hoots. Chudails young and old, in their seductive avatars and their real ones, drained towards the twins.

'Mummy, look! It's them. The famous chudails from TV!'

'Can I get an autograph please?'

'My daughter, she wants to follow your twisted steps!'

'See, they brought a delicious kitty to the party!'

'He's the Fetish Man!' Muffin announced to a chudail from Goa. 'Tried to play the virgin card and, of course, our little Jaanu fell for it.'

Jaanu slunk away, sparing a pitiful glance at the man who lay sprawled in the midst of a gaggle of curious chudails. So he wanted to massage a few chudail feet. What was the harm in that? Why should everyone always make fun of people who wanted things that were not considered 'normal'? She headed in the direction of five middle-aged chudails sitting around a bonfire, skinning cats. Cat meat roasted on makeshift skewers on top of the fire. Two of the chudails were in the middle of a heated argument.

'It's not seven, it's nine. Nine lives of a cat, remember?'

'That's just some saying, Rosy. It's seven. Go ask Granny Garam.'

'Hi Ma,' said Jaanu.

The plumper of the two involved in the argument, stopped her blade midway and cricked her thick neck.

'Jaanu! My black moon!' she cackled, scrambling up, wiping the blade against her bloodied saree.

'Is that Banal 69, I smell?' Jaanu said, grabbing her mother roughly with her claws and biting her coarse cheek.

'Yes, isn't it amazing? Muffin brought it for me. Have you met her? She and Sweety are doing a combo act in one of the movies...'

'You're looking absolutely horrid tonight,' Jaanu interjected.

Ma's face crumpled in delight. 'Did you hear, Princess?' She turned and beckoned Aunt Princess, who had been eavesdropping with her long elephantine ears. 'See, how sophisticated my daughter's become. Soon she will be the most infamous chudail in Mumbai.'

'Not really, I...'

'I'm famished! Where's Grandma?' Sweety strode in their direction, opening her mouth to expose her bottomless pit of bad breath. Muffin followed, dragging the Fetish Man. His head lolled. Dark patches that looked suspiciously like blood formed on his chest.

'Did you play vampire with him, Muffin?' cried Jaanu.

'Jealous are you?' laughed Muffin. 'It's the kitty party, Jaanu. And this little tiger has landed willingly in our laps. Of course, we had to. Anyway,' she handed him over to Jaanu and, making a face, said, 'he wasn't that tasty. Ugh.'

'Who's he?' asked Jaanu's mother, as Jaanu tried desperately to keep the man on his feet, and, failing, let him slump on the ground.

'Jaanu caught a male kitty who loves stinky chudail feet, Rosy Aunty,' smiled Sweety.

Jaanu threw her a look.

'Ooo. Really?' exclaimed Darling, a voluptuous chudail, walking up to the group. 'How quaint. Does he have anything...' Her eyes went to his groin.

'Nah. Flatter than a squashed snail. And the blood's rather ugh,' said Muffin.

'Pfft. These city types. Polluted they are. Maybe Granny Garam would like to play with him a little. She's making catrum!'

'That's the only saving *totka* in this party,' laughed Muffin.

'Stop it all of you!' cried Jaanu. 'I told you, he was here by accident. We can't *use* him tonight. Poor thing. Ma, I won't be responsible for any barbaric acts...'

'Did you just say 'use' him?' Muffin screeched, '*Use?* It's his wet dream to be suckled by chudails.'

'Oh, just wait, Jaanu. Don't start your whatchamacallit – ' Darling stopped, frowning.

'Philo-philo,' laughed Sweety.

'Philosophy, Darling Aunty,' said Jaanu. 'It's a well-respected field. However, being kind isn't taught in a philosophy class. It's…'

'It's all that education she got in the city,' nodded Princess. 'One of the *pichal*s told me it makes your hair grow inwards.' She ran her claws through Jaanu's short bob.

Jaanu ducked away, saying exasperatedly, 'It's called a haircut, I'll have you know.'

'Come, Jaanu,' said Darling, grabbing her by her arms, 'let's drink Granny Garam's catrum and then do all this philo-phallus.'

The group of chudails started to glide deeper into the island, walking under an artistic canopy of thorny shrubs. Jaanu sighed, turning to see two robust chudails dragging the Fetish Man. Poor thing.

The meandering path opened up onto another glade, where four ancient chudails sat around a bonfire. The oldest of them all, Granny Garam Badan, sat in the middle, her silhouette cut into shrapnel by deep shadows. Unruly long hair, every strand of it strikingly white, fell across her shoulders and moved like dead rats' tails as she kneaded cat flesh in a bucket with her toes, making squishy sounds and singing an ancient devotional song for Ma Chudail, her wrinkled breasts swinging in rhythm.

'Look who's come, Garam!' cried one of her companions.

Granny Garam turned and flashed a gumless grin.

'Jaanu *jaan!*' she rasped.

'Yes, yes, you're all for your Jaanu only,' cried Muffin, crouching to give Granny a nice, big bite, her saree slipping off her ample cleavage. Sweety and Jaanu did the same. 'She brought you a gift.'

Muffin beckoned the two chudails who had been carrying Fetish Man. They swung the unconscious body in front of Granny Garam Badan.

'He's going to add spark to our catrum!'

'There's enough hatred in the world...' started Jaanu

'Oh, enough of that! Here...' said Jaanu's mother, shoving a hollow thigh-bone with catrum in it under Jaanu's face. 'This time, for the party, Granny harvested male virility from the highlands of Mongolia. The hard ones, not these soft, pudgy things in the plains that call themselves men these days. Though, now that we have him, we could – '

'No, Ma. We have to think of being kind,' cried Jaanu. 'And, actually, I can't have this,' she said firmly, giving the deliciously sour-smelling catrum back to her mother, 'I've become vegan.'

'What's that?' said her mother with a frown.

'Isn't that that newfangled trend in the city where you can't eat anything and slowly starve to your death?' asked Princess, rubbing her rotund ears, 'Honey was saying – '

'It just means I don't have milk or any ani – '

'No cat's milk in that,' stated Granny Garam, giving her a cavity of a smile.

'...or animal meat, Granny Garam.'

'No meat. Just kitty blood and piss with a pinch of that yummy Mongolian white,' said Darling, smacking her blackened lips.

'Nothing that is from animal or man,' said Jaanu gently.

'But what else can you eat then?' asked Princess, frowning.

'Vegetables and fruits.'

'Hahahahaha – oh sorry, I thought you were joking,' said Princess. The twins giggled.

'Have, have. Good for the brain,' said Granny Garam, pushing the bone-cup back towards her.

'She is a philo-phallus, Granny Garam,' said Darling. 'She thinks like those silly chudails who are encouraged by that tantric fellow on TV to...' Her voice dropped to a whisper as she said the next words, '...*go straight.*'

'Straight!' cried Jaanu's mother. 'That devil of a...'

'Actually, that's not correct,' said Jaanu. 'He's a New Age philosopher who has revealed a new path for chudails who can't connect to chudailism.' There, this was it, this was her moment. It was now or never.

'And I've decided to go straight too,' she announced.

All the chatter and cackling around them fell into a deadly silence. She took a deep breath. There was no going back now. She pulled up her saree to show them ritual marks. Blackened charred stains around her ankles that marked the beginning of the Final Sacrifice – after which she would become a Straightener, the chudail that follows the forward path. Yes, that's what she wanted. To lead a normal life. A life that was normal for *her*. That's how it was going to be...

'Over my dead body!'

The entire gathering turned to look at Jaanu's shrieking mother, her claws dramatically placed on her ample bosom.

'Err... You're undead, Ma. I don't think that's going to work,' Jaanu said warily.

'But why would you want to do something like this, Jaanu?'

'So I can be normal, have a normal life.'

'You *are* normal!'

'No, I'm not. I can't even go to a library to study or an office where I can work from. I always have to sneak in – be it my college or office – hiding my feet with fake-forward shoes, putting a charm to cover how I look. It's exhausting.'

'An office? Is that a good place to find lonely men?' asked Darling, her eyes gleaming at the thought.

Jaanu rolled her eyes. 'That's not the point, Aunty. I don't want to find lonely or horny men, or scare them out of their minds, or take their virility. It's just so repetitive and banal. I want to work in an intellectual capacity, have a career which doesn't involve attracting men and scaring them witless and then unjuicing them.'

'Muffin, can't you find a job for her in a film-shilm of yours?' said Jaanu's mother, eyeing Muffin who was gulping down another round of catrum. 'Bollywood accepts chudails as they are, you know.'

'Those roles are dwindling…' Jaanu cried before Muffin had a chance to respond.

'Ohh, that is too good a joke,' cackled Darling. 'When has Bollywood's womb been dry for chudails? The men there love us. They even call their women after us. In my generation all a chudail had to do was to show herself to that horror-genre fellow – what was his name, Princess?'

'Ramray.'

Jaanu sighed as Darling and Princess began to chatter about the good old days. The Ramray Brothers, the top Bollywood horror film-makers in the seventies, had made them and a few other chudails famous by giving them important roles in their productions. Her entire generation had grown up on tales of the golden age of chudails in Bollywood.

'That era's gone, Aunty,' said Jaanu. 'Now there's just too much competition from humans.'

'Humans?'

'Haven't you heard? The new villains in the films are not chudails, but real women made up to look like us,' she said unhappily.

'But how do they turn their feet backwards? That's imposs –'

'They have computer-generated effects to do that now,' said Sweety. 'Muffin and I are even thinking of taking up roles of human villains in normal soaps since the horror roles for chudails are drying up. I hear vampires are also in vogue.'

'*Hai, hai*. Computers can suck souls, I've heard,' cried Princess, crossing her feet to ward off evil even as Jaanu's mother wrung her hands frantically. 'You chudails stay away from them. Both of you, you hear me?'

'Exactly, Aunty,' said Jaanu, feeling like she was finally getting through the thick, rough skin of her family. 'I'm trying to tell you that I'm done being a chudail. There's no future in it. I want to go straight, wear formal clothes, go to an office, buy an apartment, marry someone nice.'

'Jaanu! NO! Marriage is slow death!' cried Muffin.

'And what will you do once you leave chudailism?' asked mother.

'I will become a human resources manager,' said Jaanu.

'Human resources? That sounds yummy,' said Darling, licking her lips.

'Human resources is *not* about finding men, Darling Aunty!' answered Jaanu, exasperated. 'How do all of you have a one-track mind? It's about managing humans.'

'The juicier, the better...'

'Why would you do this to yourself, Jaanu?' her mother shook her head in despair. 'Why can't you just be normal?'

'What *is* normal?' Jaanu cried.'Look at this man, this man you are calling Fetish Man. He loves to massage chudail feet. Why can't he? Why must we all be horrid to him for his simple desire?'

At the sound of his name, Fetish Man woke up quite suddenly and jerked into a sitting position. Darling crouched in front of him, running a claw on his cheek. 'A bit dry, these city men,' she said.

'Jaanu *jaan*'s right,' rasped Granny Garam, trudging from the bonfire and hitting Rosy on her head. 'Chudails do what they want, Rosy. You forget how you hated being a chudail and wanted to turn into a man, like this one?'

'*You*, Rosy Aunty? Really?' burst out Sweety, her eyes popping out of their sockets.

'Oh, you won't believe how she experimented,' cackled Darling, even as she continued to lick the terrified man. 'Tempting men only to check out their wardrobes and the things they kept in their bathrooms –'

'Shut up, Darling,' said Rosy, kicking her sister in her ample buttocks. Darling fell over next to the horrified man, cackling. 'As if you didn't want to become a…what was it, Princess?'

'That half-fish, big-booby thing.'

'A mermaid?' exclaimed Jaanu incredulously.

'Yes, exactly,' said Princess, shaking with laughter. 'We caught pneumonia waiting for our feet to turn into flippers off the Mediterranean coast.'

'Exactly,' rasped Granny Garam. 'All of you had doubts about chudailism and all of your made a choice. Now Jaanu has to choose.'

Grabbing Granny by her shoulders, Jaanu bit her blood-covered cheek, pulling away reluctantly from the delicious catrum flavour that came off her.

'You're the best, Granny,' she cried, glancing at the man who had been watching the group, drained of all blood. 'You wanted to massage *junglee* chudail feet, right? You're not the only one whose desires are unfulfilled. Here, Granny, give him your feet and let's check out what he has to offer.'

'What *re*, Jaanu. That's not fair. We wanted to play with him,' said Muffin, her voice slurring a little.

'I brought him, Muffin. I decide.'

As Granny Garam Badan pulled up her dirty saree to show her never-washed, never-covered, twisted ancient-bark feet, delight spread like butter on Fetish Man's face.

'Oh! Thank you, Jaanu-ji, thank you!' he sniffed, reaching out to touch Granny Garam's toes as if they were hot jalebis. Granny Garam giggled as the man touched her feet with his pudgy hands.

Jaanu's mother sighed dramatically.

'Fine, Jaanu, if that's your choice. Remember, it's going to be very painful.'

'Well, giving up things is always painful,' said Jaanu righteously. 'You just need self-control.'

'When are you going to make the Final Sacrifice?' asked her mother.

Jaanu smiled as she leaned forward and bit her mother's cheek. 'I'm glad you see it my way, Ma! It's next week... Tuesday.'

'And what about the feet?' cried Princess.

'She's a philo-phallus,' said Darling. 'She doesn't mind her feet being twisted and tied up.'

'That's the problem with chudails today,' said Jaanu. 'They don't want to change. So what if the Straighteners make you wear shoes or heels. Yes, it's a bit constricting...'

'...nastily sweet smelling...'

'...and I would have to get used to walking...'

'...with feet facing *forward*. Who wants that?' cried Darling. Then she turned and asked 'Why, Fetish Man...' The man looked up from massaging Granny Garam's feet, his eyes dilated with pleasure, 'Would you want a chudail with feet pointing forward and smelling of those whatchamacallit sweet stuff?'

'Aiiiii!' he cried, taking his hands off Granny's feet and clapping his ears, face twisted in horror. 'Please don't make them straight! These...' he looked lovingly at Granny's ancient feet, 'these are just perfect feet.'

Jaanu laughed. 'Don't be silly. Of course, they wouldn't cut off my feet. That's just a rumour. We are all just scared of things we haven't experienced.'

The chudails looked at each other.

'Jaanu, I don't think you know this, but,' her mother gently put a claw on her shoulder, 'the Straighteners cut off your feet and sew them back on, backwards. The way human feet face. *That's* the Final Sacrifice. There's a reason it's called "going straight".'

'Of course not!' said Jaanu with a laugh. 'Being a Straightener means promising the community to walk the straight path, the forward path, the path of progression. It's a spiritual path toward normalhood for chudails. That's what Tantric-ji preaches.'

The older chudails looked at each other and burst into cackles.

'What's wrong with you all,' cried Jaanu. 'I'm telling you they won't cut off my feet. That's not even possible.'

'...calls herself a philo-phallus...'

'...falls for the oldest trick in tantric books...'

The women were on the ground now, rolling and laughing and cuddling the few cats that were left alive and uneaten. Granny Garam Badan burped, patting Fetish Man. She got up and clomped towards the cauldron and began to stir a fresh batch of catrum.

'Come, come,' hollered an ancient chudail, her sharp voice cutting through the chaos. 'It's almost midnight. Time to start our dance for Ma!'

The chudails glided in the direction of Granny Garam.

'Umm....Miss Jaanu –' Fetish Man whispered as the other chudails headed towards the cauldron and started their jiggle. He fished out a smartphone from his pocket, 'I – I just wanted to say...your aunties are right, you know. I've met the city chudails who took the Straightener way. See, here on my WhatsThat group. They all have their feet facing *forward*.' Jaanu peered at the screen, frowning, as the man continued, 'Why do you think I came to this island, desperate for a *junglee* chudail? Now that you've given me the chudail of my dreams,' he turned his head, looking at Granny Garam lovingly who was moving her bosom jaggedly, 'I'll never leave her side.'

Jaanu's face darkened as she realized her own naiveté. She looked towards the far end of the glade where her family, all drunk on catrum, danced and cackled. Their feet twisted and turned, thumping them rhythmically on the ground.

Granny Garam called out to the Fetish Man, who immediately bolted to her side. The delicious scent of catrum sneaked into Jaanu's nostrils, making her nose hair tickle. She sniffed at the air, eyeing the mug her mother had kept by her side. She picked it up, staring deep into it. She felt like an idiot, falling for an obvious scam – most people in the family seemed to know about it, and she hadn't even suspected! There were questions to be answered, vengeance to be taken and new pathways to explore. However, it would not be tonight.

'Oh, well,' she said, taking a large swig from the mug. The warmth of the catrum snaked through her throat, falling warm into her belly. She took another swig, emptying the mug and headed determinedly towards the circle of the dancing chudails. Through the cacophony of drunken laughter, Granny's orgasmic barks rose into the thunderous skies.

At least someone had found their normal, thought Jaanu, contentedly eyeing Granny and the Fetish Man. She thumped her backward-facing feet on the rough floor, crouching and starting to dance with her cousins.

The night was young and it *was* a kitty party after all.

# THE CARNIVAL AT THE EDGE OF THE WORLDS

## SHVETA THAKRAR

'Come one, come all! Watch all the great love affairs through the ages played out before you! Romances that transcend space and time, death and division!'

The barker stood in front of the ornately canopied theatre, clad in a shiny red-and-white striped saree. She tapped the ground with her curved wooden cane and tipped her wide-brimmed straw hat to passers-by. All around her, stars rained down in blues, whites and silvers; leopard cubs danced to guitars played by tangle-haired dryads; and a parade of feather-and-sequin-clad dancers sashayed, brilliant as rainbows, through the aisles.

The Carnival at the Edge of the Worlds had existed before time began and would continue on after time ended. Bordering all worlds, it drew all manner of travellers, offering brief and unpredictable access to entertainment as varied as its visitors. Anything might happen here – from contests to string Lord Shiva's bow to shadow wine-sampling booths to giraffe skalds trading epics in an ongoing duel and, of course, performances at the legendary puppet theatre, The Glory of the Heavens. From her perch on the stage inside the theatre, Prajakta, the *kathputli*, saw it all.

A breathless group of visitors appeared from the glowing cityscape on the horizon and converged on the theatre. 'Two minutes to showtime!' shouted the barker, punctuating the words with her cane. 'Some things are too good to be true. But not puppetry!' She collected the group's tickets, then ushered the eager patrons into the theatre.

Inside, the clamour of the outside world became a distant murmur as the doors closed, the stage lights came on and the puppets stirred to life. The air shimmered as the night-blue velvet curtains parted. Tonight's show, *Nala and Damayanti*, retold the tale of two lovers separated by distance, passing messages back and forth through a sympathetic swan messenger.

The role of Damayanti was one Prajakta had played many times. She'd been crafted for it. It was all she knew, if indeed, a puppet could be said to know anything. The marionettes with their wooden bodies and brightly painted faces twisted and danced, unseen hands guiding them from Nala's kingdom to Damayanti's, until a white curtain came down, and shadow puppets representing four angered demigods appeared silhouetted behind it.

When the curtain rose again, Damayanti, dressed in red and gold, sat on a swing beside her parents' thrones and studied the group of potential suitors before her – the human Nala and four demigods disguised to look like him.

Prajakta held on to the golden chains of her swing and smiled at the puppet playing Nala. This tiny respite, as they gazed shyly into each other's eyes, as Nala knelt beside her and sang a song, was a chance for the audience to breathe, to sink as deeply into the tale as the characters.

But just as she raised her hand to beckon Nala closer, the other puppets froze. The haunting bamboo flute playing in the background broke off mid-strain. Even the puppeteers became as still as statues.

Words sparked in Prajakta's head. *Something's wrong.*

An instant later, the doors flew open, as if flung aside by invisible hands, and wind roared in and rushed at her, a whirl of screeches and black and brown wings. She'd never been able to think before now, let alone move on her own, but somehow she shrieked and jerked free of her puppeteer.

The invading bats paid no attention; instead, they tugged her swing free of its golden stand and hoisted it into the air. Prajakta's enamelled seat rocked back and forth, but she clung to the chains the bats held aloft. She was a marionette with articulated joints, wooden limbs and a string that allowed her to be manipulated and positioned. And yet, lungs she shouldn't have possessed heaved, and a heart that most certainly shouldn't have fit in the solid bulk of her chest thumped in terror.

Before the bats cleared the theatre, a black cat sprang out from behind the left-hand door and leaped into the air, much higher than it had any right to. Its green eyes caught Prajakta's as it landed next to her on the swing, nearly knocking her off. 'Meow,' it said innocently. She gaped and gripped the chains even tighter, and then they were outside. Even with the warm yellow sun bright overhead, the bats flew on as intently as if it were night-time.

The Carnival at the Edge of the Worlds was both tiny and enormous at once, depending on where a visitor stood. For Prajakta, who had never left the theatre before, it threatened to swallow her whole. Her aerial caravan soared into a troupe of dancers dressed like peacocks, and, for a minute, everything was blue and green and violet with bits of gold woven in. She stared at it, overwhelmed.

Smells she'd only vaguely noticed before wafted over her in vivid notes: caramel apples and corn dogs and masala peanuts; sweet, sticky neon-orange jalebis. The stomach she shouldn't have rumbled. A shiver went through Prajakta. She was alive, and for the first time, she could try all these things.

But the cat must have had its own plans; grabbing her in its mouth, it jumped off the swing and into the crowd. Ignoring her protests, it herded her away from the oblivious tourists and performers with their tree-trunk legs and boat-sized feet that might have trampled her, into a gap in the traffic. Then the cat released her, batting Prajakta with its nose, and slowly, implausibly, she grew larger. She laughed in delighted disbelief as her limbs stretched out and thickened.

Once she'd reached human size, the cat brushed up against her ankles, nudging her towards an open tent of blue panels studded with silver crescent moons. She stepped inside and saw herself reflected in rows and rows of mirrors. Some made her seem larger, some smaller. Some made her appear long and scrawny with orange skin and a green stem that sprouted from her head, and in others she disappeared altogether, replaced by a creature with beautiful patterned wings or a hag with charcoal-coloured teeth and claws and dark red eyes.

She could have stared forever, as entranced as the humans communing with their altered selves all around her, savouring the sensations of existence. But the cat didn't let her. It nosed her through the winding maze of curved, convex and concave mirrors until she reached the final one. There, instead of her reflection within the silvered glass, was a waxy reddish scrawl, presumably written with a lipstick: *Just.*

*Just?* Just what?

Before she could think any further, the cat prodded her towards the exit. She frowned at it. 'Bossy creature!'

Outside, the golden afternoon had melted into a deep, dark night, all seven moons gleaming in the blue-black expanse. Prajakta realized she had been in the tent of mirrors for hours and might have stayed there forever if the irritating cat hadn't intervened.

She turned to thank her feline companion, but it had wandered off. Prajakta's gratitude dimmed like the moons before the neon signs that lit up the carnival. How was she supposed to know what to do next? She'd never pulled her own string before. Where was the hand that determined all her actions when she truly needed it?

Her eyes burned, and something wet rolled down her face. Tears! She was crying. That at least felt familiar. Damayanti too had cried upon discovering that Nala had left her in the night. Yet she hadn't given up surviving in the world.

Well, Prajakta could be like her alter ego and find out what she could about this place. Why had the bats picked her to carry away? Of all the mirrors in the fun house, the cat had pulled her to the last one. What did it all mean?

Perhaps the other residents of the carnival would know...

Prajakta waded through the visitors as they snacked, clamoured to go on rides and posed for pictures with goblins and gargoyles. A few glanced her way and started, but most were too absorbed in having fun to notice anything amiss.

None of the kiosks or stalls seemed like the right place to find answers, and she continued past them to an enormous purple swimming tank that glowed with a deep pink light. A trio of friends frolicked raucously in its aquamarine waters: a siren, a nagini and a rusalka. The siren's piscine tail and the nagini's serpentine one glistened in the rosy radiance, while the rusalka's ice-pale legs swished back and forth. All three wore delicate gold crowns studded with seashells and freshwater pearls, and smiles that would make anyone with any sense run far away.

Perhaps that hint of danger was the allure, or perhaps it was the siren's melancholy ballad, awash with longing, for visitors crowded around the tank, desperately fishing for the baubles at the bottom of the tank. Even Prajakta felt the call of the song. In her mind, it became: *Nala. Oh, my Nala, where are you?*

Sadness washed over her. She was nothing without her Nala.

But that was the play. She had no other memories to fall back on, unlike these humans who clearly searched for things they'd once lost or simply never had. She felt smaller, more alone, than ever.

Her nose twitched where the cat had touched it, breaking the spell. She shook her head to clear it. No, feeling sorry for herself wouldn't help. She had something to search for too: her identity. That was why she'd come here.

Once Prajakta remembered that, the song faded and the strange women's conversation came into focus.

'... favourite ways to lure men beneath the waves,' said the siren. She grinned, revealing teeth as rounded and white as the pearls in her circlet.

'My cousin, the foolish Uloopi, is soft-hearted and dragged a man under only to marry him and set him free once more,' the nagini hissed, and made a disparaging noise. 'Where is the fun in that?'

The rusalka, who had been stealing glances at Prajakta, now crooked a finger at her. *Come here.* Her friends turned to see what she was looking at.

Prajakta approached the tank. 'A small sister,' said the nagini, as though Prajakta were still the diminutive puppet. 'What do you want with us, little one?'

'Do you know who I am?' Prajakta asked, her heart thrumming with anticipation.

'You might as well ask what it is like to breathe air,' the siren retorted. 'Of course, we know.'

The rusalka poked her in the side. 'I don't believe puppets breathe, silly goose.' Her voice was like the flurry of the bats' wings as they'd sped Prajakta through the sky.

'I suppose not!' The siren laughed. 'Well, little one, think of it like that. Except there is also the silk and fury of the water, how it caresses you like a mistress, how it holds you like a mother, how it drowns you like a murderer.'

'She can be grey, she can be green,' added the nagini. 'She runs cold, she rages hot, and sometimes, she is a tranquil and balmy blue. But above all, she — '

'I know how to breathe. Will you tell me who I am?' Prajakta interrupted.

The women tittered. 'Go fish.'

As Prajakta watched in frustation, something flashed in the corner of the tank, green and intriguing. It looked like a gemstone, its facets reflecting the tank's pinkish light, and twinkled with the promise of information. *Prajakta*, it called.

Prajakta stared at it, forgetting everything else. She needed that jewel.

Now she understood the siren's song of yearning. Impatient to answer, to reach the disc, she clambered up the side of the tank.

The humans on either side ignored her, intent on their task. One huffed his exasperation and tossed away his fishing line to reach directly into the tank. Two scaly, muscular arms reached back and pulled him under.

Even that couldn't deter Prajakta from her goal.

'What are you doing, small creature?' the rusalka keened. 'This game has rules.'

'Stop!' said the siren and the nagini in unison. 'You can't come in here.'

Their words drifted right over Prajakta. She dove in, then broke the surface of the warm water and bobbed along, determined to get to the glittering bauble.

Seaweed, crabs, eels, banks of coral and darkness assaulted her, scraping, clawing, clipping. The seaweed knotted itself around her, but she stretched out her arm – just that much further. Just an inch more – until her fingers closed around the object.

The tank's inhabitants hauled her out and tossed her to the ground, drenched and still wreathed in seaweed. Then they too crawled out, lips pinned back to reveal daggers where teeth should have been. Instead of heeding the threat, Prajakta stared at the word sparkling on the emerald disc. 'A,' she read aloud.

Pain shot through her in forks of lightning and flame. The nagini had sunk her teeth into Prajakta's shoulder. She cried out and tried to pull away. The nagini was quicker, and slithered back with a chunk of wood between her teeth.

Prajakta clutched her wounded shoulder. Was this what being alive was like? This constant agony? 'I just want to know who I am!' she exclaimed.

'Everything has a price, little sister,' the rusalka rasped, while the siren snatched the disc back. '*Especially* knowledge. If you wish to know yourself, you must be ready to endure the pain.'

The siren trembled with wrath. 'This tank is for the foolish and the arrogant. They come to us, proud and spiced with greed, and we eat them. Anything that invades our waters becomes our prey. *That* is the price of knowledge.'

Now even the humans stopped their frenzied treasure hunt to gawk. The nagini hissed, and they quickly resumed fishing for the missing bits of themselves. 'Are you pleased with what you have learned?' she asked Prajakta. 'Was it worth the price?'

*Yes*, Prajakta thought. *It was.*

'Leave,' whispered the rusalka, while the siren sang to cover the sound. 'Leave before we're forced to finish consuming you.'

She didn't have to say it a third time. Prajakta darted off, her thoughts centred on just two words.

*Just. A.*

*Just a.*

Just a *what*?

She only stopped running when a three-storey tall ogre and a fancily dressed asura blocked her path. 'A puppet, free for the taking!' The ogre's meaty hand descended and closed around her.

'Let go of me!' Prajakta snapped. Her blunt wooden teeth did nothing against her captor's rough green skin, and she made a face at the taste of salt and dirt on her lips.

'Now, now,' he grunted, 'play nice, or I'll pull your little string and make you dance. *Dhoom-dakka-dakka-dhoom!*'

'How about you let her go?' suggested the asura, who, in contrast to his companion, was well-built, even handsome. 'We have no time to play nanny to a lost toy.'

The ogre continued as if his friend hadn't spoken. 'Good thing you got us to look after you, don't you think?'

*Hardly*, Prajakta thought and glanced around. She would have to rescue herself if no one else would.

A nearby pink-and-gold canopy advertised a take-a-shot gallery. The players aimed their guns at shooting stars and fired to the tune of an unseen calliope, but the stars were harder to hit than they looked, starting out slow and then blurring across the backdrop that was the night sky. The ogre watched them with obvious hunger.

A cluster of prizes hung like wisteria from the gallery's ceiling: an inflatable orange snake with a live toad in its mouth, a fruiting apple tree and a giant, dirty, hole-ridden pair of boots. Odd prizes, to be certain, but they reminded Prajakta of Nala's second wager with his brother, where he reversed the loss of his wife and kingdom by putting Damayanti up for stake. Instead of Nala risking Damayanti, however, Prajakta would risk herself. 'Where is the skill in finding a stray puppet on the street? If you want to impress me, win that pair of boots,' she challenged.

The asura scowled. 'Those filthy things? Why would I want to?'

'Do you mean to tell me you *truly* haven't heard that no one dresses like you anymore?' Prajakta wrinkled her nose at his silk kurta. 'All that lush cloth and rich embroidery? That's gauche and *so* last year.'

The asura exchanged his scowl for a smirk. 'I don't believe you.'

That was fine with her; he wasn't the one she'd been trying to trick. 'Fine, don't believe me. But you can at least admit that neither of you has any real chance at winning the boots.'

Now the ogre bent his head to peer at her. 'Of course, I can. Silly little puppet.'

The asura crossed his arms. 'Don't listen to her, *bhai*. She's trying to make you look like a fool.'

'What do I have to lose?' the ogre replied. He flexed his free arm until the biceps bulged. 'No one can best me.'

'Then,' Prajakta said sweetly, 'you won't be afraid to enter into a little bet? Win the boots and you can keep me. Lose and tell me who I am. That is, *if* you know.'

The ogre's eyes widened with glee. 'Who *doesn't* know? Oh, this will be easy!'

'I'm telling you, you'll regret this,' insisted the asura. 'You'd do better just to let her go now.'

'You know, you're such a spoilsport. Sometimes I think you don't want me to have any fun,' the ogre grumbled, pouting.

Prajakta turned pitying eyes on him. 'Does he determine your fate, or do you? Some scary monster *you* are.'

'Give me a turn,' the ogre growled at the vendor. The asura shook his head but said no more.

'I'm sorry,' said the vendor, 'but the minimum play is three tickets.'

'Three it is,' said the ogre. 'Even though one shot is all I need.' He transferred Prajakta to his left hand, thrust three tickets at the vendor with his right and took the gun.

The vendor pressed a button, and the music began. Stars shot across the sky. Even holding Prajakta tightly, the ogre took out all 10. Then the next 10 from his second ticket and the third set of 10 from his last.

Prajakta's hope dwindled like Nala's had when he despaired of never being able to make things better for Damayanti.

The vendor applauded. 'You're a ringer. I didn't think anyone would ever claim — I mean win — these boots. Well done!' He took the boots off their hook and passed them over the counter along with the snake.

The ogre put Prajakta down to try on his new boots. 'Wait, what about the tree? Don't I get that too?'

'Oh, I'm sorry,' said the vendor, 'but for that, you need to win another five games.'

Five more tickets were slammed onto the counter before the vendor had finished speaking.

The asura threw up his hands. 'You'd think you would have learned not to gamble like this after I had to buy back your freedom last time.' The ogre, engrossed in his game, didn't react. 'Go home,' the asura muttered to Prajakta. 'You're just a story.'

*Just a story?* Prajakta's mind didn't understand immediately, but her heart stuttered with recognition.

'You belong on the stage. Shoo, go home.'

The pain the nagini had mentioned burned through her as Damayanti's voice echoed in her head: *Nala! Where is my Nala? I must find him.*

*Just. A. Story.*

Leaving the ogre and the asura to their fate, Prajakta ran back to the theatre, where the cat who had launched her from the swing waited with the barker. 'Is it true, you fickle creature? Am I just a story?' she asked.

The cat meowed, though it sounded more like a honk.

The barker tipped her straw hat. 'Is any story ever just a story?' she murmured, her voice low and strange, an invitation. She led Prajakta and the cat into a familiar place – Damayanti's palace from the play. The courtyard teemed with suitors, guests and the royal court. The *svayamvara*.

It had to be true, what the asura had said: everything Prajakta felt belonged to Damayanti – her pining, her resolve, her devotion. Everything she remembered was one of Damayanti's recollections.

Nala approached them, clad in yellow and green, and only then did Prajakta realize that the rest of the scene was immobile. 'Thank you sincerely,' he told the barker, who inclined her head.

'I know what it is for stories to rot with misnarration,' the barker said.

'What about me?' Prajakta demanded, fighting against the joy and affection swirling in her heart at the sight of Damayanti's hard-won husband. They weren't hers. 'What's going on?'

'My dearest wife,' asked Nala, 'do you truly not remember? Stories change through time, with the teller and the audience, and our tale – yours and mine – was in great danger.'

Prajakta shivered, gooseflesh rising over her as though she had skin. She couldn't say why, but his words resonated deep inside her.

'The details slipped and shifted until finally you chose one of the demigods and not me, and that threatened to replace the truth,' Nala continued.

A glimmer of memory flickered within Prajakta. 'And erase it,' she whispered, both frightened and excited. 'Erase...us.'

Nala nodded. 'It was your idea for us to be stored in the bodies of these puppets, re-enacting our true story until it had regained the power to be rescued from the shadows of obscurity in our world.'

'Only in the carnival,' said the barker, 'which stands outside time itself, could you halt further decay, so you asked me to help.' She gestured at the cat. 'Show her, friend.'

'You have served me well – as ever,' Nala agreed. He crouched down to stroke the cat's head and its black fur elongated into fluffy white down. Soon, the cat had become a graceful swan.

'Come out, dear Damayanti,' Nala urged. 'It's safe now.'

'I'm… I really *am* Damayanti then?' Prajakta asked faintly.

'Yes,' said the swan. It hurried over to her side and gently pecked at the wound the nagini had inflicted, then touched Prajakta's string. 'May I?'

Prajakta pressed her lips together. She had only just found out she existed. What if the swan pulled her string and she ceased to be? Not the puppet Prajakta, not Damayanti, nothing? Something tugged inside her, like her heart was splitting in two. No matter what the swan said, she couldn't help but believe she would vanish.

'You awoke now because you have finished your task. The true story has regained its power, and it is time for us to return to it,' Nala said. His smile radiated love. 'Now, will you return to me?'

The tugging ceased. Yes, she would. 'If this is going to happen, I need to do it,' Prajakta told the swan. It nodded and backed away.

Feeling like she was about to leap from the airborne swing once more, but this time with no cat to cushion her fall, Prajakta squeezed her eyes shut. If she vanished, at least she didn't have to watch it happen. She reached up behind her and pulled the string.

Everything spun as the cosmos realigned itself. The puppet's memories of the day gave way to something bigger as wood turned to flesh. They expanded interminably outwards, images slotting together like pottery shards: Watching her parents preside over the royal court, nibbling on pomegranate seeds and sipping sweet nectar from golden goblets, handmaidens weaving jewels into her long, wavy hair before she met with friends to trade in the currency of confessions and daydreams. Meeting Nala.

Then it was done.

Damayanti opened her eyes to find herself leaning against her husband. Her red-and-gold saree, heavy with gems, complemented his dhoti beautifully. 'I think we should start with a trip to the theatre,' she said, caressing his cheek, 'and after that... Well, we're at the edge of all the worlds. Why not visit each one and learn their stories before we return to our own?'

The barker handed her a piece of paper shaped like a tree. 'This is your evergreen ticket to watch all the plays you like,' she said. 'You've earned it.'

'If you don't mind, Nala,' said the swan, 'I think I might like to roam around here for a while. Being a cat has made me curious.'

To Damayanti, Nala said, 'You found your way back to me. You saved us. I would deny you nothing.' To the swan, he added, 'Enjoy yourself until we meet again.'

Then, ticket pressed between their interlinked hands, the lovers strolled away while the barker rapped her cane on the ground and announced the theatre's next run of performances.

# THE RAKSHASI'S
# ROSE GARDEN

## SUKANYA VENKATRAGHAVAN

The neighbours talked a lot about the occupant of 606 A wing. For one, she was so beautiful. No, attractive, according to Mrs Munshi of 606 B wing, because 'she is dark, no?' Dark but attractive, everyone agreed.

Also, nobody knows when she comes and goes, Mrs Sharma griped.

What does she do all day?

Nobody knew.

She looked great for her age, there were no quarrels about that. What a gorgeous, curvaceous figure! But, wait, what was her age? 25? 32? 40?

Nobody knew.

They watched her from their balconies and windows as she seemed to wind up and down the pathway, draped in jewel tone sarees, her long hair sometimes open, at other times tied in a thick braid, her skin the colour of a summer sunset, a certain sorcery glowing from within. They really couldn't tell the colour of her eyes – they may have been black or even a hazelnut brown. Mrs Iyer, who fancied herself a writer, once described them as 'deep, like the turbulent ocean'. But that could mean her eyes were green or grey, or perhaps even a deep blue.

'Maybe she wears contact lenses like those actors in serials,' said someone, and everyone nodded. Maybe.

No one could remember how long she had lived there. She may have told them but they had forgotten. All of them. And now it was a little embarrassing to ask. Neither could they be sure if she owned the flat. It was the largest apartment on the top floor of the building. The only one with a terrace – the terrace. With the rose garden.

The rose garden was a particularly popular topic among the ladies. How the flowers, mostly roses but a variety of others, all quite magnificent, seemed to be in perennial bloom. How they were bigger and more beautiful than any others they had seen. How they never seemed to fade.

'How come they never fade?' asked Mr Munshi once. 'What manure is she using?'

'Maybe it is some foreign brand,' said Mrs Sharma.

'Maybe she talks to them. They say, *na*, plants grow better when you talk to them.'

Everyone had fallen silent after this exchange.

It was Mrs Munshi's turn to host the monthly high tea and even though 606 A was invited, she didn't attend. Not that she ever did. The ladies didn't mind because this gave them a chance to talk about her over tea and samosas.

They had all been gifted blooms on their birthdays through the year, and Mrs Khanna had once taken a flower apart petal by petal to check if it was made of plastic.

They had all waited for a couple of weeks and then quietly thrown away the still-fresh flowers. Mrs Sharma had stuffed the blooms into a polythene bag and tied it up tightly with a number of rubber bands before throwing it into the garbage bin because she thought they had started to *whisper*. In the dead of the night. Sometimes in the sleepy quiet of the afternoon. Occasionally at dawn...

This was, of course, Mrs Sharma's little secret. And Mrs Munshi's. And Mr Iyer's, on the third floor. And Mrs Khanna's. Because who wants to be told they were imagining things or needed their ears examined?

The thing the ladies talked about the most, though, was the men.

'So many of them.'

'No shame at all.'

'Changing boyfriends like panties.'

'Always someone or the other coming and going.'

Mrs Sharma frowned, a line of doubt appearing on her forehead. 'Well...no one has actually seen them *go*? Isn't it? I only see them come to her flat.'

'Must be leaving early morning. Who knows?

'Maybe having wives also.'

'Her appetite is something else, *haan*.'

And all of them laughed. A little nervously. But that wasn't because they didn't like their neighbour in 606 A. They just didn't understand her, and because they didn't understand her they were a little scared of her. Pity, because if they had mustered up the courage and just asked Ira Second-name-unknown, the neighbour in 606 A, she would have told them the truth. About her age, the roses, the men...

Only, they would have forgotten the second after.

For instance, she did tell Mrs Sharma that she was 6,000 years old and still preferred her former life deep in the forests to the concrete jungle she had chosen to inhabit for the last 200 years. Mrs Sharma will not recall this because that is how Ira meant it to be. The old lady had passed out after the information had been shared with her, not just because she knew deep in her tired old soul that Ira was speaking the truth but also because she had looked into the Rakshasi's eyes and seen it for herself – the forests, the wild magic, the rivers of blood... The pain had been too much to bear, and she fainted. When she came to, Ira was sitting next to her, with a cup of tea, telling her gently to keep a check on her blood pressure. After all, she was getting on in age, wasn't she?

The year before, at Mrs Munshi's birthday party, Ira had told both Mr Munshi and Mini, as she was called, on their little balcony, that her entire family had been slaughtered by a king. He had wanted that part of the forest to build a lodge for his hunting grounds and the Rakshasas who had settled there were loathe to leave. This had made the king furious and he had sent a band of soldiers to persuade the Rakshasas into leaving. They had refused. Ira spoke of how she alone had escaped death because she had gone hunting. She had returned to find her village up in flames, her parents dead and disembowelled, and her siblings missing, possibly hauled away to the kingdom to be the king's slaves. They were too young to use their magic and by the time they would come of age, it would have been beaten out of them. Mr and Mrs Munshi nursed their gin and tonic as Ira told them how she had sunk to her knees and wailed, and the moon had slid out of sight for it could not bear her anguish. The next morning, the couple had woken up with excruciating headaches; doubtless, the wine was to blame, they told each other.

So, you see, if you asked Ira she would be more than happy to tell you everything about her life, including her rose garden. But no one ever asked her about the garden, because after all flowers were just…flowers. For instance, right now, she was in her balcony, absently smoothening the creases on a rose petal, as Nikhil the banker told her all about his life, including the girl who had accused him of raping her when all he had done was be persuasive.

'Come on, man, if she didn't want to fuck me why did she ask me back to her house?'

'I can think of a couple of reasons,' Ira said.

'What is a weak no? It's a yes.'

Ira's eyes lit up with some kind of ancient rage as she told him why it was not. She told him how the king's men had taken her, all 14 of them. Grown men, laughing as one took the place of the other while her cries gradually weakened. She told him what she did afterwards, and watched as he started shaking, sweat breaking out on his forehead, trickling down his face. By the time she was done she knew he would remember forever. No, Nikhil the banker did not deserve the kindness of forgetting.

An hour later, in the wing opposite, Mini Munshi's increasingly fickle bladder woke her up and she muttered her way to the bathroom. The little window in the loo directly overlooked Ira's flat. Force of habit made Mini peep through and she let out a low *aah* when she saw Ira in the balcony, pressing mud into a pot that contained a new rose plant. Her long fingers disappeared into the soft dirt and emerged again, nails painted scarlet, as deep as the roses in the garden. She was in a saree, black and gold, a mirror to the sky and waning moon above, humming a strange melody under her breath.

'She is beautiful,' thought Mini grudgingly for the millionth time before she reluctantly finished her business and went back to the bedroom.

'Who gardens at midnight? That girl is very weird,' she told Mrs Sharma the next morning. Yet, when Ira arrived at her doorstep with a little bunch of roses for Mini Munshi's daily puja, the older lady accepted them without comment.

'Diwali is coming soon my dear. What plans? Any family coming down?'

'I don't have any family,' said Ira, smiling. 'I have told you this, Mini, don't you remember?'

Mini Munshi flushed a deep red and stuttered her way through an apology. Later she texted Mrs Khanna on WhatsApp: *No family. That's why so many boyfriends.*

*Poor girl*, came Mrs Khanna's reply.

Ira came back to her flat, her skin tingling with memories that Mini had so unkindly brought back, of mud lamps in huts, meat roasting in a spit by the river, and laughter. The laughter haunted her more than anything else. She wandered into her terrace barely noticing the eager whispers of her blooms. The memory of laughter slowly churned into the smell of burning flesh, the distinct scent of terror and the excitement in the eyes of the men who had returned to the village to look for survivors. They had found her by the river, babbling to herself, cold and alone. They had taken her back at their commander's order and thrown her in a dungeon by herself. She repeatedly asked them about her brothers and sisters, and all they had done was laugh.

'You are actually a disappointing lot,' one of the older guards had said. 'I can see none of the Rakshasa magic you are famous for.'

She didn't tell him that the magic kicked in only when you were older, 14 at least. She didn't tell him that hers had, on a new-moon night after her 13th solar turn. A strange, weak magic that she distrusted and disliked. Wasn't magic supposed to be powerful? Wasn't it supposed to make her feel *something*?

'Ira, your magic won't have any effect unless you tie something to it. Some feeling of passion, some strong emotion,' her mother had told her, keen eyes watching her impatient daughter struggle with this newly awakened force.

'Right now, all I am feeling is irritation,' Ira had replied, gripping a dead twig with all her force. It crumbled into ash and fell to the ground.

'Be patient,' her mother had said softly. 'Your magic knows when to take shape.'

Her mother was right. It did. That evening the guards dragged her out of the dungeon into the wild, neglected garden. They had each had a turn with her, spat on her and told her she was ugly. She could barely move, let alone stand, but had staggered to her feet, a fistful of earth in her hand. The men had stopped laughing because they saw it in her eyes, the wild flare of magic, the freshly wrought rage that would not die over centuries, the inexplicable power, visible though her brokenness, electric and terrifying. She had thrown the earth at them, and there was a second when nothing happened. Then the men vanished, and in their place stood cacti, ugly, thorny, rooted forever in their violence.

Ira had fallen to the ground, shattered both by what she had just experienced and the electricity that was coursing through her. By the time she could pick herself up, the palace had been alerted and she could sense a hundred men running in her direction, sweat, adrenalin and fear coursing through them. When she finally left, the palace grounds were silent, covered in blood and mud, with cacti and creepers speckling its every inch.

Her siblings were dead. She had looked for them and found them in a dungeon far down the corridors. Gone before they could access the magic they were meant to channel. She took them out into the garden and left them as sunflowers, bright, blooming and smiling wildly at the setting sun.

She hadn't been able to save them. She hadn't been able to protect herself. What was the use of this magic, she had wondered for decades, as she woke up from nightmare after nightmare, alone, cold and angry. What was the use of power if you couldn't use it when you needed it the most? Then she had begun to understand, as the familiar rage showed in other situations, where at its peak, she was at her strongest, the magic spilling out of her like a thunderstorm. She didn't know how to control it and she didn't want to. Her mother's magic had been music. Her father's was linked to love. Hers was just rage. And she finally understood. You couldn't explain magic, or the fount it sprung from. You could only use it in the way you best knew how – and so she did.

Rage was her magic.

She lived through time, creating wild blooms out of her anger, her sorrow. She left behind entire cities of whispering flora, mysterious gardens, alive with the men who let her down time and again, who betrayed her, who couldn't love her back the way she wanted them to. She thought of the men who had cursed through the ages without a second thought, turning women into vines and rocks, kings who had banished their queens, wives punished for their desire, daughters sold off in brutal barters... She was all women. Their heartbreaks and violations were wounds in her own body and soul, and the collective experience a turbulent river bounding through her veins.

Rage was her rose garden. Wild, strange and whispering. Never fading.

The whispers seemed louder this dark moon night. She plucked a few jasmines and threaded them onto a string. She looked at herself in the mirror as she braided her hair, studding them with the starlit jasmines and the faintest whispers.

'What are you looking at?' she asked her reflection. 'What do you see? Do you see Medusa or Circe? Do you think I am worse than them, or better? Don't you see I am stronger than Ahalya and Sita, Urvashi and Shoorpanakha? Do you prefer Kannagi or Draupadi to me? Would you rather that my rage was fire, burning down cities? Or a stare turning men to stone, anger that transforms them into sheep?' The reflection stared back, eyes devoid of the rage that had burnt within her for centuries.

The doorbell brought her out of the reverie. It was the new neighbour on the first floor. Her six-year-old daughter was missing. Ira shut the door, the mother's panic fluttering in her own heart. She knew, she had always known. But she had never had proof. Girls missing for hours. Girls coming back different, blank-eyed, never the same again. She held on to the panic she had borrowed from the mother. It would take her to the girl. If she was lucky, she wouldn't be too late.

She stepped out of the house, into the lift and down into the dark basement that used to be the car park. It was now just a dark dank place below the building where its residents 'stored' their junk.

She had been late many times before, only finding the child, alone and terrified. This time she saw him with the girl. There was a look on his face that Ira instantly recognized when their eyes met. Fear, maybe defiance; not shame. She had known it was him for over a year now. She hadn't done anything because she hadn't wanted to arouse suspicion.

She didn't say a word to him as she reached for the child. It took her only seconds to speak to the girl and send her home, the girl's memory slowly fading and rearranging itself. All she would remember was that she had wandered off. The mother would let it go after all, faint with relief that her daughter was back. Mr Munshi, on the other hand, Ira thought to herself, would remember forever. He would make a spectacular geranium.

The girl returned with only a few minor bruises and a missing memory, but everyone was too relieved to mind too much. She was alive, she seemed unhurt and most of all she seemed okay. But now Mr Munshi was missing. He had been last seen going out for a walk the previous evening and had not returned. Mini Munshi had stopped eating and her friends now gathered around her, holding her hand, muttering conspiracies under their breath. If Mini had been keeping her usual watch on Ira, she would have noticed her in her garden at midnight on the previous night. New pot, new plant, new bloom.

Weeks passed, and the conspiracy theories around Mr Munshi's strange disappearance reached alien-abduction level. Mini Munshi, meanwhile, was slowly attempting to move on. For starters, she successfully resumed reports on Ira and her activities. 'New plants. At least two or three,' she told the others. I saw her watering them and singing to herself at midnight on Tuesday.' The others nodded, relieved that Mini seemed to be herself again.

When the doorbell chimed, Ira knew who it was. She had been expecting this. In a bid to 'move on' and 'be normal again' Mini Munshi had taken to visiting each of her neighbours in turn, every day.

'Hello my dear,' said the older woman as Ira opened the door. Mini looked a little thinner than she had been a month ago, but her eyes were alight with curiosity.

Ira invited her in. 'How are you?' she asked gently.

Mini Munshi winced. She had no idea how to answer this query.

Ira grasped the older woman's hand and Mini felt a strong surge of emotion. Alone, puzzled, thrown off her routine as a wife of 35 years, *relieved*? Ira felt the woman shuffle this thought as it appeared, and shove it to the back of her head. It was hard for her to accept.

'Shall I make some tea?' asked Ira. She didn't wait for an answer. Soon, water was boiling and some strong floral tea was brewed.

'I usually drink masala chai but this is so nice,' muttered Mini even as the tea soothed her brain, letting her sink back into the couch, relaxed. 'It's new for me. Mr Munshi, he only liked *adrak* chai.'

The squeals of children playing outside in the building compound filtered in through the open terrace doors.

'He loved children you know. He always went downstairs to play with them. This is the time of the day I miss him the most.'

Of course, Ira told her everything. How she had suspected for years, how clever Mr Munshi was in never getting caught, how she finally did catch him. And what she did to him. Everything. As the sun set outside, flooding the apartment with its tangerine beams and lighting up everything, including the whispering flowers, Mini Munshi forgot what she had just been told.

'You were saying something, Ira? I'm sorry, the tea was so soothing I...I lost track...spaced out... That's what the kids say nowadays, no? Even Maya used to say it all the time. Until she...left. You know, for college abroad. She is so busy she hardly comes now.' Mini Munshi trailed off a little breathlessly.

'She never visits. I know why. So do you Mini,' said Ira quietly. Mini looked up, stricken, the sticky secret salt and water in her eyes for a brief second and then vanished. The tiny blip in her memory made her head lighter and she looked around, trying to focus.

'By the way,' she said airily, wondering why her eyes were watery all of a sudden, 'you have some new plants I see. I saw you gardening the other day.'

At midnight you mean, thought Ira. Though you will always see only what you want to see.

'I do have some new plants,' she said brightly. She pulled the geranium out from her hair. 'This is the newest. It is blooming beautifully.'

She got up and tucked the flower into Mini Munshi's hair. The older lady patted her hair consciously and smiled.

'I hope you don't mind that I did that,' said Ira softly. 'It suits you...'

'No, no, I don't mind,' said Mini Munshi. 'Mr Munshi always liked *gajra*s in my hair, any flower actually. I wish...I wish he could see me now...'

'Perhaps he can,' said Ira sincerely. 'In fact,' she continued, as she went to the terrace, picked up the blue ceramic pot of geraniums and came back into the living room, 'why don't you have this? I feel like it belongs to you.'

A low whispering that seems to emanate from the terrace tickled the air in the room.

Mini Munshi began to protest, when Ira said very softly, 'I feel like it is what Mr Munshi would want you to do. Since he liked flowers.'

Mini took the pot. Caressing the flowers, she said, 'They are very beautiful, thank you, Ira. I hope they won't die in my flat. I am not very good with plants.'

'I promise you these won't,' Ira said, her tone comforting and sincere. Mrs Munshi left, holding the azure blue pot of newly bloomed geraniums that had begun to whisper ever so slightly. She would put them on Mr Munshi's desk, next to his photo, she decided.

Ira walked onto her terrace, the sky incarnadine, speckled with birds and clouds. She walked around, touching one bloom and then the other. She plucked a rose, young and eager, from its stem and tucked it behind her ear.

'Perhaps one day I won't feel the need to do this,' she said to the roses. 'Perhaps one day I won't need a rose garden.'

Her phone dinged a notification. She glanced at it and sighed. After a few seconds she said to her roses, 'I don't have enough jasmines in here. I should go out and get some jasmines.' Then she picked up her house keys and walked out, a strange song in the ripples of her hair, leaving the garden alive in operatic whispers.

# BAHAMEEN

## ASMA KAZI

lides of a broken heart. Chopsticks. Glass animals. A dozen polka-dotted sketch pens. Candles. Candles. Candles. Lavender. Lime green. Rose. Sticky notes. Sticky notes. Hot pink. Electric yellow. Pocket mirrors. A yellowing newspaper clipping from five years back: 'Forty-nine Babies Die in an Indian Hospital Due to Lack of Oxygen'. A visiting card: *Bahameen Scahbaaz, Creative Director, The Ad Guys.* A recipe card, filed under N for *nalli-nihari.*

I scan through my belongings in the room, making sure we have everything for the fire ceremony tonight.

*Let go. Let go. Let go.* Between chants of letting go and feigning excitement about the new that is still unknown, I feel like a mere shadow of myself. We gather around the fire once every blue moon, sometimes a blood moon, sometimes a wolf, when the stars in the sky seem to be the farthest away and lack lustre. We sit in ceremony to release the toxic and the dilapidated, when the otherwise therapeutic ripping of old bills isn't enough and the need to destroy that which won't work anymore is immense. How often is too often for a ceremonial release, I wonder. When is it time to let go of the constant need to let go?

Not anytime soon, I think. We are such suckers for drama. No matter which realm we come from, it is always the same. In case of an emergency, break glass, set things on fire. Rinse. Repeat.

The room smells one part week-old cologne, one part freshly brewed coffee and two parts dense, like you could run a knife through it and slice off a neat chunk of the void. The letting go is heartbreaking, but the prospect of seeing the old, glitchy narratives sparkle, fizz and go up in flames has us all excited. If you were there you'd be excited too.

\*\*\*

This realm is built on stories. It is dense with mythology, a collection of myths, each different, depending on where and when you were born. Stories on which they design their religions. Stories about Smurfs, Tweety Bird and Iron Man. Stories from architectural dig sites and galactic viewing, of the beginning and ageing of the universe.

Some of these stories are based on fact, some are wanderings of an over-imaginative mind, all luscious, stacked one on top of the other, their juices melting into one another, creating new layers. Some layers are rigid, while others continue to flow, finding new rivulets to blend into, becoming new tales. Fact or fiction or something in between, gray; you may lose track of which is which.

When you are a time-jumper, though, it doesn't matter. If you listen carefully, you can imagine it, you can also tap into resonant imaginations of the other time-hoppers. When you see it all clearly, the imagined and the unimagined, you can hop through the temporal portal to wherever the story in your head takes you, no matter the era, or whether it is real or fiction. It doesn't matter which land, what galaxy, or the multitude of tales within that galaxy. You just hop to it.

*\*\**

It has been 200 days since I time-jumped. It is getting more and more difficult to stay in this one place. I have to, though. Every time I have jumped time on this Blue Earth, I have lost a reality. It feels like a lifetime, leaving me a little shallower of experience and with the counter reset to zero-zero-zero. This deterioration of memories was set in motion when I began to involuntarily time-hop. At the time I was 25 in earth years, still a teen in hopper years. It is the gravity on this planet and the amalgamation of tales that emerge from the land that really mess with the time-hopping experience. Standard temporal hopping rules do not apply here, and everyone who jumps time in this realm is differently affected by it. The effects of these time-hops, sometimes in a butterfly effect, also cascade into other universes.

On one particularly glitchy day a couple of moons ago, a fellow jumper named Reeba came back from her travels beautifully tanned from the Atlantian sun and sand, with a blue hand where her nose was supposed to be. A boy in Pandora woke up that morning, after a night of astral travelling, to discover a rosy nose where his arm used to be, and panicked. He thought it was the Sphinx's and feared he would suffer the curse of the Great Sphinx of Giza.

We had to call in our high priestesses and time doctors from multiple realms, to look into the anomalies and recalibrate everything in accordance with Blue Earth's rules. There was a ceremonial broth, and we added a nose of the Sphinx to this one. If you were wondering, neither *nez du* Sphinx nor Sphinx was harmed in the making of this broth. There was some furious incanting, an unfurling of knots and glitches, a setting right of timelines and there reappeared a nose on Reeba's face, exactly where it was meant to be. With much gratitude, bowing deep, twice, never gazing into her enchanting eyes, we returned the borrowed nose to the ever-gracious Sphinx.

Meanwhile, in Pandora, oblivious to the ceremony on Blue Earth, the blue boy was convinced that the Sphinx's vehement dislike for unidentified flying objects had brought her wrath upon the boy, and he vowed to abstain from astral travelling over the Sphinx ever again. He hoped that this would be enough to pacify her and coax her into returning his missing arm. And *POP*, just like that, there it was, his beautiful blue arm, like it had never left.

For a time-hopper, everywhere is home, and nowhere is. As part of the initiation into the time doctor's council, I had to live a lifetime on Blue Earth.

The rules for me on Blue Earth, as part of the initiation rites, required me to leave all my time-hopping memories behind. I'd live on the planet like I was of this planet, like it was my first ever lifetime here. I was, however, allowed to pack with me three Blue Earth avatars, reminders of my time-hopping and other lives, to help me navigate through the gorgeous and most treacherous lands on the planet. I carried these avatars as orbs of light – red, blue and yellow – inside me, hidden from the Bahameen me. They would reveal themselves, with tidbits and cheat codes, at times — whenever the circumstance got dire and I needed them — as survival mechanisms. Then they would be me and mine, and stay till the end of this lifetime.

When the time was right I would remember it all, and my initiation would be complete. After the remembering and a ceremony to clear out the debris of stagnant plots and grating subplots, would begin my task of setting right the particularly dense storylines and all things anomalous in this land and others.

***

I was born three decades ago on the day of the spring equinox. My mother named me Bahameen, which in Pahlavi, ancient Persian, means 'spring'. I was her beautiful day after the long cold winter had passed. I carried within me melodious bird songs heralding the arrival of good days.

Being born on a day when the day and night stretch to meet each other as equals, I also carried within me the burden of constant resurrection. Of seeing parts of me crumble away every night like eraser dust, and rising every morning from the ashes. It was like being addicted to being a phoenix.

This is the realm in which the first of the time-hoppers was born. Most time-hoppers on the Blue Earth were women. A story from this realm suggests the first of us was born from the rib of a man, there's a story before that, a story of us being moulded from dust, and another of us arising out of fire. The rib, the dirt, the flames, a black hole, all figments of someone's imagination. The womb of this Blue Earth is where the first story was born — the story of the Blue Earth, of time-hoppers, of other earths, and other kinds of temporal hoppers; stories of enchantment.

This here is the story of a rib. The story many times multiplied, mutated, seeped into timelines not of its own origin. Not restricted by its own plot now, and open to interpretation, it plays havoc as a new version on an alternative timeline.

*Once upon a time, there was a rib. A rib displaced from its original story. They walk this earth, phantom men missing phantom ribs, always seeking to fill the void, looking for their ribs incarnate. There is seeking, sometimes as warm and fuzzy manifestations, and tales of everlasting love; twin flames and candyfloss weaves emerge. At other times the search commences aggressively, as unthinkable violations, and is stuck in an infinite loop of world dominion by a rib, and the ritual of burning at the stake those who remember for the appeasement of a rib that doesn't remember or fit anymore.*

Most of us, the new hoppers, are from breakaway plots and different lands. We live a life of wading through the rich storyful bogs on Blue Earth at least once, as a rite of initiation into becoming a specialist time-hopper, a time doctor in my case. We sometimes visit here when the glitches arise and there is need of intervention. For me, this visit has been a bit of both. I'd tell you more about the land I was born in or all the lands I have lived in since, but this right now is one wee story, a little bit of a story of an already little one, a wee story of the Blue Earth and me. I'd tell you other stories, the elaborate ones that go on and on for eternities, or the shortest of short ones that start with 'once upon a time...' and immediately hop onto '...and they lived happily ever after', but those are stories of another time, for another time, waiting patiently to ripen to their full glory and have their time in the limelight.

\*\*\*

Tara, the Red. She came to me easy. She was all heart and roses and popping candy. An until-then dormant fragment of my personality, she was my astral-travelling, *chaat*-loving, yogini self. Tara appeared to me like the joy of sparklers at Diwali. Triggered, she came to me as the feeling of death, and then the calm of bobbing up through red-hued depths after being forcefully pushed into a water tank, headfirst, at Holi. She came to me as all things boisterous and enchanted, and all things the keep-your-head-down-and-stay-modest-me feared and did not yet understand.

This Tara-that-was-me was braver, more trusting than the original Blue Earth me. She was also the reason I had the ability to fly-kick-drop, Bruce Lee-style, as and when I needed to. She was a good addition to my mostly well-behaved, sometimes passive aggressive, hip-hopping Bahameen self.

I was born a non-believer in a land lush with tales of elephant-headed gods and ten-headed anti-gods. Playing a multilevel maze game where everyone around had a cheat code and a way to reincarnate, keep coming back, while I had to get it right the first time or burn in the fires of hell for a hundred years, and a few hundred more. Tara revealed to me the cheat codes I needed, and a way to navigate this maze. The codes came as residual cellular memories of high priestesses, hula-hooping and the Divine Feminine. As magical codes, a whisper in the wind that had all this while been trapped, awaiting acknowledgement and its time in the spotlight once again, like Aladdin's Jinn. I have always loved the loopholes in fairy tales. There is always a way to break the curse. A fairy godmother, the prince or a toad, there's always a portal to the happily ever after. Tara brought to me a way to break my own curse; she showed me how to remember through my dreams.

As I slept, my dreams came visiting, and every dream awakened me some more. The dreams that I once never could recall on waking up now spoke to me as I slept. I saw the minutest details of everything it showed me, my old memories from a life at a place most home-like, from life at the many lands I had lived in. It was my personal bioscope to the world of the animate, and every day I saw the picture a little clearer than the day before. The day came soon enough when there was not even an iota of doubt, and I had remembered it all.

Ari and Shimona. Blue and Yellow. They are my vegetarian personas. They appeared much before Tara. Before the dreams, before the Remembering, I called them memories of me from another lifetime. I called them a coping mechanism, a way to deal with a many-fragmented personality. I filed them under the woke-up-one-morning-and-could-play-the-piano-or-speak-a-foreign-language-with-no-logical-explanation category.

Ari and Shimona came bearing gifts from Atlantis and Ancient Egypt. Memories of giant rose-quartz crystals, dust storms and aubergine *shwarma*. (If you are ever so fortunate as to find a place that serves you an aubergine *shwarma*, ask for an extra dash of *toum*. Never skimp on the *toum*.)

The goon squad has been doing the rounds this past week, going from door to door demanding that people make good choices. This has Shimona in a tizzy. They have been inspecting garbage bins and online profiles to track what everyone in the neighbourhood is up to. Like bloodhounds, they're sniffing out all that does not comply with their warped definition of 'a good choice'. The different sounding names, the likes of the Khans, Kanes and Kenzos are on top of the list.

Shimona is in one of her contemplative moods this morning. Can one ever outgrow the effects of her name, she wonders.

Maybe we should have chosen a different one. Maybe things would then be easy. It is after all the earliest label that probably affects the development of you in ways you cannot even imagine. How your name rolls on another's tongue. How it affects you every time it is said right. How it influences your persona when the *a* in your name is replaced by the sound of *ohm*, transforming a lovely day in spring into a bout of bohemian rapture, anxiety and breathlessness all rolled into one. Every pronunciation, right and wrong, like little blows shaping up the form and destiny of you.

There is a burden to being born with a name too different from the rest of the populace, one that never lets you fit in, one that always prompts the other to ask, 'Where are you from?', one that never lets you belong.

That is also possibly one of the biggest downsides to travelling through time and living in various realms; you never quite fit in. Even when you live in a land which is the only land you remember ever having lived in, when it is the only home you know of, deep down in the core of your being, your inability to fit into the larger narrative annoyingly ticks on.

***

Coming back to where I started...

There's a broth on the menu for the fire ceremony tonight. In the good old Blue Earth days when the goon squad hadn't taken over the neighbourhood, we cooked a beautiful bone broth, a soupy *nalli-nihari*, particularly warming on a cold night, which worked just as well every time one needed comforting. A beautiful broth eaten with chunks of warm, freshly baked bread. *Delicioso!*

But the goons, they took away the steak, the bones and hide. When it came down to a choice between steak and the stake, we chose vegetables. We skipped the firepit.

'Okay girls, only mandrake roots tonight, no more real-baby cries, we don't know what will set those goons off... Also, no cheeseburgers at the girls' night in tonight,' Ari and Shimona declare in unison. They are thrilled about the vegetarianism, though not so much about it being forced down our throats. Tara and I are definitely not thrilled about soya pulao. There will be the ceremonial broth, of course, although, sans the *nalli*, a tad bit less dramatic, with unmagical 'shrooms and blahbloid carrots. We also consider cooking a beetroot rasam this time, it would call for some major tweaking of the ceremonial broth recipe, it would call for some very difficult-to-procure-items – tears of the gold-spotted fly catcher, the plant and not the bird – from Mars, to dissolve all the woes, but it would be a gorgeous red, and maybe, just maybe, just as spectacular. We add glass eyeballs, Indiana Jones-style, to the broth sometimes, and pretend we are the exotic monkey-brains-eating-eyeball-soup-drinking-white-people-appropriated-version of how folks from this side of the world are supposed to be. It is unrelated to the ceremony, but we do it just to hear the vegetarians in our home squeal. The girls shine the brightest and the most beautiful, like the aurora borealis, when they are freaked out like that and on the verge of falling to the floor, rolling, laughing. That's their superpower, being sparkly, like raindrops hitting the palms of one's hand, like a chilled bubbly tingle on a parched tongue. Our home is never dark for too long thanks to this pair of glow bugs.

A *nalli-nihari* night at Chandni Chowk beckons, of *khameeri roti* dunked in endless comforting, greasy bowls of greasy broth, *daal tadka* and *paneer tikka*. We will do a girls' night out at the dhaba tomorrow after the girls' night in tonight, maybe. But no more bone broths at home. The last time we did so, we spent a few hours worrying about the bones showing in our garbage, then travelled across multiple state lines in the course of the night, to the end of the galaxy, trying to dump the bones without seeming shady.

Here is the recipe now, only for the brave.

## NALLI-NIHARI

Prep. time: 15 mins
Cook time: 90 mins
Total time: 2 hour 15 mins. An eternity, maybe.

*Ingredients*
- Half kg leg of lamb, aka *nalli* or *paya*
- Two teaspoons ginger-garlic paste
- A pinch of existential angst to cancel all angsts, from Rasfatariana
- One heartbreak, your own
- One teaspoon turmeric powder
- Salt, to taste
- Half cup cooking oil
- Two bay leaves
- Four cups sunshine
- Half-inch piece of a cinnamon stick
- One tomato
- Three onions
- One teaspoon cumin seeds
- A dragon scale for courage

- Two green cardamoms
- Five cloves
- One glove
- A chunk of fool's gold, to taste
- Nutmeg, preferably not more than a pinch, but go by your instinct
- Half teaspoon black pepper powder
- One teaspoon red chilli powder
- One teaspoon coriander powder leaves and stardust for garnish

*Instructions*

1. Wash the lamb pieces till squeaky clean.
2. To slow-cook lamb add one chopped onion, turmeric powder, one existential angst, half teaspoon salt, quarter cup oil, one teaspoon ginger-garlic paste, cardamom, cinnamon, fool's gold, a glove, bay leaves, the cloves and one and a half glasses of water in a cauldron.
3. Cook on a high flame for 15 minutes, whistle, stay in tune, whistle the 'Bohemian Rhapsody'. Lower the flame, tone down all pent up outrage and cook for another 60 minutes. Switch off the flame and let the pressure settle. Breathe. Ooohm.
4. Bring out one more onion. Hulk-smash it. Breathe. Again.
5. Grind four cups sunshine, cumin seeds, the smashed onion and one heartbreak to make a fine paste. Grind some more, till the sun shines through.
6. Put on your rose-tinted glasses. Heat the non-stick pan with remaining oil and temper with bay leaf and all the residual angst. Make sure you get it all this time.
7. Add one chopped onion in the pan and fry it till light golden in colour. Add the ground paste.

8. Add to it a dragon scale, chopped tomato, red chilli powder, black pepper, coriander powder and more salt, *andaaz se*. Cook the spices on low flame till oil separates. Hop.

9. Add the spice mix into the cauldron along with a glass of water and a wee sprinkle of nutmeg. Mix it well. Check salt; if needed, add more salt. Cook for another 10 minutes on low flame. Whistle. Again. Dance.

10. Switch off the flame, let the pressure settle down. Garnish with coriander leaves and a sprinkling of stardust.

11. Serve hot with fresh-baked bread, *kulcha*, *naan*. Share with a group of friends. For the broken-hearted, it will set the pieces all right; for everyone else, it will add a little magic to life.

Feel the warm and fuzzy yet?

***

Recorded baby gurgle bombs, like yarn bombs. Like the tales from the ancient fort, set on full-moon nights, when one can hear the cries of a boy betrayed by his own uncle, calling out to the man to save him, '*Kaka, mala wachwa!*' We are setting the sound bombs off by the now-abandoned hospital tonight. The sinister gurgles sans babies are meant to be a reminder for us and for them, the baby killers, of the fateful day when 49 babies died at this very spot, and the cataclysmic effects of which reverberate through us up to this day. Today, however, no babies would be harmed in the conjuring of this illusion.

Time-hops, fire ceremonies, love potions, crystal grid woowoo and gurgle bombs. That is all we do. Never blood magic. That's an absolute no.

The baby killers were other people, the goons. They didn't even bother to do it under the guise of faux rituals on a new-moon night. Just deemed the babes different, sucked the oxygen right out of the tanks, replaced it with methane from their cowsheds and sent the silver canisters to their Ministry of Cows. Their bossmen wear gold grills and sit as tall as their riches-inflated bellies will allow them to on their oxygen-tank thrones. This faction believes that the resources in these lands are dwindling and that Blue Earth is dying. A group of large corporations is already in discussion about monetizing the water resources of the world. The goon squad believes it's keeping ahead of the curve by hoarding on oxygen supplies, their idea of setting claim on an essential resource they believe will also eventually deplete. They raid hospitals and low-security oxygen cylinder factories to source the oxygen tanks; they have become quite the menace.

As ludicrous as the idea is, of depleting oxygen and stashing tanks, it is an idea they believe in without a doubt, and who better to deprive of resources in the present in order to secure a possible lucrative future than the ones who already seem different. Groups like these will always identify someone as 'different' and expendable. It starts with those who appear to them as being at the other end of the spectrum and finally ends closer to home, *at* home even. The goons, I once called them 'wolves in sheep's clothing'; but they actually are sheep, evil sheep in wolves' clothing.

When you walk by the hospital on some new-moon nights you can see blue babies floating about, just by the overhead water tank. They don't cry. Don't stare. They just float there, mid-air. With their eyes shut, mouths taped, as a reminder, lest we forget. They send chills down your spine, just like the haunted cries of the boy betrayed on a full-moon night.

These sections of the story from Blue Earth are like the bog. They are the most ancient and most hostile to any kind of new and non-kindred. They are like lumps in the broth that didn't mix right and mutated into something ogre-esque, something much bigger and different than the original broth itself. These bogs can be very draining on time-hopping and time-hoppers. Moving through these channels is like wading through lead and it is best avoided. Being the original fount from where all stories emerged, Blue Earth is where you'll find most of these bogs, and the resultant time-hopping anomalies. The characters like those from the goon squad and its likes are similarly rigid, like the bogs they emerge from, and hostile to anything and everything even a little different from the narrative of the bog.

\*\*\*

'Forty-nine Babies Die in an Indian Hospital Due To Lack of Oxygen'.

The memory seemed important to the Blue Earth Bahameen. In an attempt to set a storyline right, my first after the initiation, we used the newspaper clipping from five years ago as a portkey. We hopped back in time to just before the goons took away the oxygen tanks. We were able to thwart the attack, the babies supported by the tanks saw another day and more new days. Forty of those babies survived and grew up to be healthy, beautiful adults: the timeline was set right. On another earth this kind of resetting would have worked without incident. It would have been our '…then they lived happily ever after'. But here, in this realm, it created a parallel timeline and the baby-killing events multiplied, sprouted like poisonous wild 'shrooms in hospitals across the world. One also in a city outside the galaxy.

This is the first and the last time we tried to change a past event on this earth. We had someone else to blame the first time, now there was no one but us to blame, in an attempt to set things right we had just worsened the situation. Some time-doctors are of the opinion that in a time-travel paradox it was this event and the setting right of it by my future self that had also triggered an anomaly in my timeline of involuntary time-hops and memory deterioration. This was unexpected; it was horrifying. We learnt quickly how the more one resisted something on this plane, the more it persisted – and aggressively so. We learnt to focus on correcting what we could with the currently running plots and some proactive clearing to avoid anticipated new anomalies; we learnt to breathe and wade through.

***

I don't remember time-hopping before Tara. The irony of it is lost on no one. It seems like a cruel joke, a typically Blue Earth joke that she brought me memories of my lives before this life, and just when she emerged my memories from life on this land were almost all gone.

It's been 600 days since Tara appeared, and I remembered to check the time-log. I read through it like the numerous times I have before, but I still don't remember much of the person, the Blue Earth Bahameen, I was before Tara. In the absence of my time-hopping memories my time-jumper mind had been hopping time involuntarily. To the untrained eye not accustomed to the ways of the time-hopper, it looked like I was losing time and had a dissociative personality disorder. Every time I travelled through time, involuntarily, unaware, being someone else, there were parts of my memories that just crumbled away, and I woke up every morning less and less me.

Tonight is the last time I'll have any Blue Earth memory of my own from the time before Tara revealed herself to me. I will have my time-logs and a view into the life I lived here, but I'll view it as an outsider now. In the absence of involuntary jumps, and now in control of my time-hopping experience, I'll view it as one 'cured' of a Blue Earth ailment, but as an alien to my experiences in a land that was home.

\*\*\*

Dancing away into the gray. There is a fire ceremony and a party of eight tonight. Two steps forward, half a step back, repeat. It is time for the ceremonial release, and to let go of the remnant Blue Earth Bahameen past. Time to free myself of the old glitchy narratives, of time-travel paradoxes and memory loss, and to welcome the new. A BFF. Girlfriends from dance school. A crystal-whisperer. A dragon-tamer. Two colleagues turned close friends from the ad agency I work at. Time-hoppers, all. My trusted avatars Tara, Ari, Shimona – Red, Blue and Yellow in my head. That makes a party of 12. There is a spectacular red ceremonial broth, *no nallis were harmed in the making of this broth.* There is a constant writing of notes to self. A constant writing of chants, and rewriting them, till everything piles up at the side table like a tall stack of gold and silver candy wrappers, 'You don't want to create a new crop of anomalies,' I remind myself. 'You have to get your incantations right this time.' There is a very full house, of fun, food, and setting things on fire. Some sombre letting go of the cold and the old. Reviewing. Reviving. Integrating. The many shades of spring. Bringing in Bahameen.

# THE GIRL WHO HAUNTED DEATH

## NIKITA DESHPANDE

It's only a moment's difference between ripe and rot.

That's what my Amma would always say. 'Fruits will blush with a succulent sweetness just before they turn over and die.'

At that time I thought it was, like everything else, a lesson on marriage.

As a child, I'd run from tree to tree in the palace gardens, plucking the figs while they were still green and hiding them under my bed. *If they stayed hidden from the heat of the sun, they would never ripen. Their time would never come.* Or so I thought, until I woke up one morning to a bloody mess of flesh and juice and the sour tang of broken dreams.

I sense that stench in the air again, thousands of years later, when he walks into the University campus where I teach. I cancel a lecture, make excuses and take the weekend off. All day, I sit by the window in my apartment, snipping the overgrown pink bougainvillea twined with the grill. I toss the flowers, one by one, into a wide, brass vessel filled with water and wait for the petals to age like prunes. When I find the courage to leave for class on Monday morning, the flowers have still not withered or sunk to the depths. It gives me a sort of hope. But when I put my books down on the class table and turn, he is there, sitting in the middle row, scribbling in the back of a notebook with a red-and-black-striped Natraj pencil.

Two young women in the front keep turning to look at him.

I ignore them and dive into teaching.

An hour later I am close to concluding, when his hand flies up in the air. I continue to speak, even though something in my stomach has caught spark and burst into a bright, blue flame. 'And this is the point Simone De Beauvoir is making. She says every time a woman, a female character makes a move towards self-assertion, it supposedly takes away from her femininity, her likeability...and her...seductiveness...'

I lose my train of thought as we lock eyes.

'Yes?'

He has the courtesy to look down and smile at his notebook for a moment before he says, 'This is Western thought in an Indian classroom. In our culture, the women in our stories asserted themselves all the time. Draupadi's hair left untied and dishevelled until washed in the blood of the enemy. Sita, steadfast, even in the face of fire. And who was it that haunted Death himself until he gave her husband back? Ah,' he says, his perfect bow-shaped lips curling into a smile. 'Savitri.'

The heat from my stomach jumps up to lick my face.

'Th—the women from our mythologies,' I say, stressing on the last word, 'were trapped in the complexity of their own time. And were constantly punished for asserting themselves in their own ways. It's…er…an entirely different subject from what I'm discussing…'

'But ma'am,' he interrupts, waving the Natraj pencil rapidly in the air so it looks like a trident…or a pitchfork. 'They *are* brave women. Norm-breakers. And still seen as idols of femininity in this country.'

'If you still want to pursue this debate, you can see me after class,' I say with some force, hoping I sound brusque and dismissive. But the corners of his lips curl again, like it is some sort of an invitation. I rush out of class after the bell and sit in the staffroom among the other teachers, pretending to correct papers. No matter how gentle I am, the ticks of my red pen look like slashes.

Later, when I walk out to the terrace to get some fresh air, he is there, sitting among the potted plants. The black-and-white kitten adopted by the staff purrs in his lap. My heart jumps as he turns to look at me, stroking the kitten with absurdly long fingers.

'You don't need such an elaborate ruse to talk to me,' I say, drawing the pallu of my saree around my other shoulder to shield against the strong breeze.

He beams. His teeth are mostly straight. His eyebrows thick and wormy like twin caterpillars, his dark hair, straight and windblown. He looks completely different from the last time we met and yet, it *is* Death in that white T-shirt and jeans.

'I was just curious,' he says, in a deep voice that could bend the wind into submission. 'To see what perspective you would bring to a – what was it – an 'Introduction to Gender Studies' class.'

I fold my arms. 'Why are you here?'

'As always, puppet. To see you.'

The wind whips around us, fiercer than usual. The sky darkens, its edges orange, as if catching fire. I don't miss the signs. There are few things Death loves more than spilling blood in the sky.

'Who is going to die?' I clench my jaw.

He rises to his feet and takes a step towards me. Then another, and another, until a hard, warm hand reaches up to touch my cheek. 'I had forgotten about your questions, Savitri.'

It's a trick. To call me by that name is to touch me in many different places at once.

I close my eyes. 'I have a different name now.'

'Hmm… But to me you'll always be the same 15 year old I found on a forest floor, weeping next to her husband's body, begging for him to be returned. How many centuries has it been? Do your beloved humans even know how to count back to that time? Hmm? Do *you* remember?'

*Do I?*

The stories people tell now, they once heard from their grandparents, who heard it from theirs, who read it in a book, written by a saint, who was told by five other rishis, who say they read it in an ancient text written by an elephant god.

In that story, Savitri haunted and followed Death and begged him for her dear husband's life. She impressed him with her wisdom until her beloved husband was returned to her, whole and alive.

Unfortunately, I am not that Savitri.

\*\*\*

Let me tell you a story.

Many centuries ago, I was walking through a forest with the man I had married. I was all of 15, no more a child, barely a woman.

But in a time when women did not choose their husbands, I had fought the rules of the world, just to become his companion, his most ardent servant. That was the meaning of marriage in those days. If he wanted a drink of water, I knew to read the slightest movement in his mouth so that a jug would touch his lips before a single syllable had spilled from them. They said if I was a good wife, if I was truly devoted, I could prove all the prophecies wrong.

But he collapsed one afternoon as we picked nuts and berries in the forest. He clutched his body where his heart should be, slurring words and commands. It had been a long year of prophecies and fire sacrifices. I had learned to make talismans out of salt, lemons, chillies and mustard seeds to protect him and yet when it came down to it, my husband writhed like an insect.

Then the forest went unnaturally quiet, like it was sucking in a breath. Leaves ceased their rustling. The wind turned mute. Animal calls died in their throats. The sour smell of puckering fruit was everywhere. I thought of the figs. The gardens. Fingers of the sun reaching for them below my bed.

Heart pounding, I looked up from my husband and stared straight into the eyes of Death.

A woman.

Contrary to everything I had been taught. The opposite of all that I had read and heard in stories and scriptures, she was a woman, a god, her skin as dark as cinnamon bark, teeth artfully crooked, and eyes that looked like the very heart of dancing fire. A jewel like no other – something celestial – shone from a pin in her nose.

'Please,' I begged. 'Please don't take my husband.'

'It's too late for that now,' she said, her voice full and melodious, like the sound of a woodwind instrument. 'Go home.'

'No, please. He was the only thing that made life worthy of living. Please, give him back.' I started to sob.

She circled us slowly, watching my husband like he was prey. I clutched his body tightly to my own. My tears stained his cheek.

'Please, please, give him back. I love him. Please.'

This seemed to enrage and delight her all at once.

'Love.' She scoffed. 'What do you know of love, little puppet? You go where the gods send you. You pick up glass and think it's a diamond. You slice a finger and think your heart is broken. You see one face of a brilliant, many-faced thing and you think that's all you want.'

The body between us vanished. Death closed a fist. My hands clutched at air.

'I – will – serve – you,' I stammered in between sobs. 'I will go wherever you go, do whatever you want, if you give him his life back.'

She laughed and took a step away, hips swaying seductively, a hand pulling all her long, wavy hair over one shoulder. 'It doesn't work like that.'

I followed her, convinced that if I got close enough to pry open her fist, I would find my husband. But her magic was strange and intoxicating. The forest around us thickened and dissolved into whorls of colour – deep purple and the blackest black, fiery flickers of amber and midnight blue. No matter how fast I walked, it seemed like I stayed in the same place: just inside the outline of her shadow. Only the stars remained unmoving above us, looking like a legion of distant gods, twinkling dangerously.

'If you intend to follow me,' she said, stopping after what seemed like many tedious hours, 'prepare to walk for a long, long time.'

I looked around. We were in a part of the world I had never seen before.

You have to understand. These words I use now to describe it, to remember it – I did not have this vocabulary then. I did not know, for example, that the huge grey metal monsters before me were called 'ships'. Or that the pale-skinned people going about their work, in clothes I did not recognize, were mortal, humans of another race that would descend upon my people and rule them one day.

All this I learned later, from asking.

'You underestimate me,' I said to her then, trying to ignore the new, intimidating surroundings. 'I will torment you with questions.'

She stopped in the shadows of a large vessel, turned around and laughed. Her bird-like eyes crinkled in a very human way.

'Why would I be tormented by your questions?'

'My husband...' I wiped fresh tears at that word. 'He...he used to say I could irritate the most evolved, the best learned, the most disciplined of saints with my questions.'

Death narrowed her eyes at me. It felt like I was being watched by something larger. The universe. A dark, turbulent ocean. Some great, big beast with hooves and wings, flanks and feathers.

'All right, puppet,' she sniggered. 'Consider it a challenge. If you manage to ask me a question that annoys me, even a little, you can have your husband back.'

My eyes must have widened in something like joy because she sneered, almost immediately. 'I should warn you. There is no question you can ask that would irritate me. No number of them.'

We walked on a while, cold to the bone in gloomy, grey weather, toward a towering bridge in the distance. Rats scurried beneath our feet. Everything reeked of waste and disease. I wondered where we were and what we were doing. She seemed to be in no hurry.

'What if you are annoyed but you pretend not to be?' I said, after a while. 'What if you...forgive me, but how can I be certain that the emotions you express to me are truly the ones you feel?'

'Very good.' She looked genuinely impressed and a little amused. 'Doubting the honesty of gods without an ounce of fear for their wrath? What a rare thing you are! But trust me, duckling. If you ever manage to offend me, you will know.'

She was smiling but something in her tone made me shiver. I kept my questions to myself – just for the moment – so I could watch her closely, and observe how things as simple as light and air turned at her command.

It was hard to tell how long we had been walking. Hours melted into minutes, and years into centuries into units of time man had not mastered yet. Again and again, we tiptoed across the threshold of time and space, doing a chore here, a job there. The fist opened and closed. And when it opened again, it was always empty. No part of the world was beyond Death's reach. She ended kings and children in one strike.

Sometimes, we remained unseen and I walked in her shadow, asking, asking, endlessly asking. Sometimes, she shifted shape and took new forms – a man, a woman, something in between, neither. Perhaps, I thought at one point, she was magicking new forms for me.

I was never out of place among mourners. At first, I could only see the mothers, the wives, the daughters and the sisters, familiar among the hurt and the grieving. What was it to me if they wrung skirts or sarees, hide or trousers? If they broke bracelets, bangles, beads or bone? Pain was emblazoned on their skin.

Once at a river ghat, they laid a baby to rest under a rough stone. We sat on large, rusting pipes. Death wore a man's form now, his bearded chin resting on his folded arms, staring into the eyes of the sun as if threatening it with his own fire.

The words staggered in my mouth but I asked the question.

'Where do people go when they die?'

He smiled. 'They go wherever they think they're going. Dying is a wish-fulfilment like no other.'

'So does that mean the baby is happy?'

'I didn't say that.'

He looked into my eyes, and it struck me, for the first time, how close we were sitting. If I moved my arm, our shoulders would graze. I think he noticed it too, because a few moments later he folded his legs so that our toes touched, our knees pressed head to head, like in prayer. My heart jumped, like it had been jolted awake from deep sleep.

'I think he was annoyed, not because you ask too many questions, but because you ask the difficult ones.'

'Who?' I said, without thinking.

Death grinned, a little surprised. 'Your husband?'

My cheeks burned. He turned his gaze back on the sun. But something between our knees buzzed with heat in spite of the cool afternoon. After the sun had plunged into the mountains, we dusted ourselves and walked on, and the frisson that had existed minutes ago flickered and died.

In those days, when we left one place and time for another, it felt a lot like I was being blindfolded and spun in circles. I lost the ability to tell the difference between then and now and then. Like the needle in a compass, I pointed due north every time, waking in Death's shadow, under the influence of whatever magnetic pull he had. And yet a small part of me continued to quiver, long after the spinning had stopped, as though it believed my north should be something else.

'How can it be that you have the magic to travel the world,' I asked Death once. 'And we only go to the places where terrible things have happened?'

We were in a dingy tavern. A man had just collapsed, spilling a whole barrel of wine the colour of blood. The people who were trying to run for help slipped in the mess. If I didn't know the man was already dead, I might've found it funny.

Death sat before me, drinking thick, dark mead from a glass he had magicked out of nothing. 'Terrible things are happening everywhere, all the time, duckling. Humans have the great privilege to only feel grief for what happens to them.'

'I've been wishing I had that privilege for a while now. But each one gets to me worse than the first,' I sulked. 'Don't you ever want to take a break? From the constant dying and the dead?'

'If you had the power, where would you go?'

'Somewhere bright and colourful. A place that feels...alive? And at a time when nobody's sick or dying.'

He smirked as he rose from his seat and walked out the front door, his fist closed tight. I sighed and followed him out into the wet, cobbled street. Little grains of sand rose out of the gaps in the cobblestones and swirled around us in a breeze that hadn't been there seconds ago. The wind picked up, eventually enveloping us to become our own, private sandstorm. I grabbed the end of his kurta and followed even as the sand rained pinpricks into my cheeks. When it finally settled, I could smell roasting meats and vegetables. My toes curled into warm sand. I opened my eyes.

We were standing in an enclosure of patchwork tents. Camels, goats and bulls ambled about, wearing strings of little bells in their necks. Sunlight danced off mirrors sewn into women's skirts. Scarlet and orange turbans coiled like snakes around men's heads.

A desert fair.

I looked over to where Death should have been and found her wearing the same skin she had worn when we first met. She was dressed in a large maroon patterned kurta. Her dark wavy hair hid beneath a yellow turban. The shape of her legs just showed through the thin, white cloth draped around her waist. This time when she looked into my eyes, my body rose in gooseflesh.

'Where are we?' I said, looking away.

When Death smiled, it was not soft. It was sharp and cutting. 'Somewhere bright and colourful.'

A glorious sunset seared the sky. We stopped to hear a gypsy woman sing. A scarlet *ghoongat* covered her face, so that only the bluish tattoos on her neck were visible, her voice was high and loud and gruff. A young man played the *ravanhattha* by her side, his eyes closed in devotion.

The gypsy's song boomed across the mela, rising higher and warmer than the new-born campfires, silencing boisterous goatherds, demanding the attention of sleepy camels and weary travellers.

Next to me, Death opened her fist in a small, graceful movement, like an infant's yawn.

*Please no, not the woman*, I thought. How could she silence her now, like that, mid-song?

But Death's hand waited, open, next to my own. A moment later, I understood. I opened my own fist and took her hand in mine.

'What is she singing?' I asked, leaning so that my head could rest on her shoulder.

'Her song...is a question too.' Her nose turned to bury itself in my hair. Something throbbed in a hidden part of my body.

'She says she has found every god and goddess you can name. Every kind of heaven. Every saint and sinner known.'

'So...what's the question?' I raised my head to look into her fiery eyes.

She sighed. 'Where should I go to find you, my love?'

I put my head back on her shoulder, digging into the warmth of her body.

We walked on the sands long after the fires had become puffs of ash flying on the backs of desert winds. We sat side by side with our backs against somebody's tent. I watched her skin shine in the moonlight. All this time, so many hours. She had stolen this slice of time for my joy, in a place that was alive in every grain.

I asked questions, so many of them: Could gods remember being born? This job of hers – did she think it a drudgery or a privilege? Did she always work alone? What happened during wars? And famine? And didn't it confuse her to hop across time like that? Some questions she answered and some she evaded cleverly, by leaning in, half-laughing and half-sighing into my clavicle. Finally, she held a slender finger to a spot in the very middle of my bottom lip.

'No more questions,' she said, pulling away the finger and bringing her lips to mine.

If you asked me what it was like to kiss Death, I would say it is like drinking moonlight while at the bottom of the deepest ocean, without ever stopping for breath. To weave your hands through her hair and hold the nape of her neck is to reach across the horizon and touch the part where the light never reaches.

At some point that night, I fell into a deep, honey-thick sleep, with her head buried in my chest. When she shook me awake, it felt like a century had passed.

The sun blazed down on the desert. A shriek seemed to be pulling apart the fabric of the sky.

'Come,' she said. 'It's time to go.'

There was no outstretched hand. Her fist was closed again.

I wiped my mouth and looked around.

The cry belonged to the gypsy singer from last night. Men and women tried to hold her back as she slapped their hands away and clung to the fallen body of the young man I had seen playing the *ravanhattha* last night.

Her son, perhaps?

I stared.

'Puppet. We should leave.'

I looked up at her, my eyes brimming over. She had done this to our *somewhere bright and colourful*.

I shook my head. 'No.'

She had looked surprised. Or hurt. I remember thinking it was a trick of the light. Moments later, she turned heel and walked away.

And I ran forward to do the only thing I knew. I pushed past the crowd and held the singer's head to my bosom and listened to her wail against my beating heart.

*\*\**

Death and I take a bus out of the university town. It's hot and rickety, and every inch of the vehicle squeaks and creaks as we make our way down bumpy roads.

He leans his head against the bars of the window and begins to sing aloud. It's a sad song from a movie in the local tongue. I look at him in surprise. At first, his singing earns him a frown from the bus conductor and a man trying to nap behind us. But some of the women watch him with shy smiles. Some nod along to the tune.

I go against everything in my being, every lesson I've learned, and watch. I watch how his eyes remain closed when he sings. His long lashes. How his hand automatically goes to his chest, just where his heart should be, when he hits the harder notes and the truer words. When we get off and walk toward the beach, I find the courage to take his hand. He raises a bushy eyebrow at me, but I walk, pulling him into my shadow.

It has been two decades (and half a lifetime) since that desert fair. I was found, taken in, paid for, violated, then saved. I was taught language like they teach apes and babies. I was fed and re-fleshed. I built a simple life out of learning and teaching. His arrival has made ripples in that life. But I still enjoy the warmth of that hand in mine.

We buy spiced peanuts in newspaper cones. I eat hungrily. He plays football with kids in the sand. We find a small coffee shop in a narrow lane. We lean against the whitewashed brick wall. He pauses to close his eyes and inhale the smell of the coffee in his steel tumbler before drinking from it.

'Why did you choose to come here?' he asks.

'I wanted to be near the sea,' I say.

What I don't say is this: *The people here have the same dark, coconutty skin you did when we first met. They have quaint superstitions about you; they think if they sleep with their heads toward the south, you will arrive. They say tentative things like 'I'll be back' instead of final things like 'Goodbye'. They rarely wear black. They paint red-faced demons on their doors to chase you away.*

'Why did *you* choose to come here?' I ask him.

I want him to say it was me. I want some muscle in his human face to betray whatever affection brings him back to me, time and again. I want to see his hand fly to his heart like it did when he sang that song.

But there's a moment's hesitation, and it gives him away.

'Who is it? Who's going to die? Not one of my students?'

'There was a girl in your class today… This is not some kind of personal vendetta against you, you know.'

I put my tumbler of coffee down by the shop door and tuck 50 rupees underneath. I don't wait for change.

He catches up with me in the next lane. Before he can stop it, I push him up against a wall. I can see in his eyes that he isn't surprised by the force of it, but the closeness bothers him. I lean in to let my nose nuzzle against his neck, trace the hard line of his jaw.

'Take me,' I whisper. 'Spare whoever it is and let me die.'

He pulls his head back and smirks. 'I told you ages ago, puppet. It doesn't work like that.' He brings up a fingernail to scoop the tears streaking my face.

'You've grown so much. I thought you would see enough faces of the diamond to stop being blinded. But look at you. Still bedazzled. Still thinking your life is worthy in exchange of some...human's.'

I pull away, shaking my head in disbelief. 'Why do you, of all people, look down on love?'

'Love, attachments – they're mortal weaknesses. Haven't you noticed how much humans suffer on their account? Haven't you suffered?'

It cannot be. The person standing before me can't be the same person who sang a song of separation and longing on a bus three hours ago. He cannot have known the real meaning of the gypsy woman's song in the desert.

'So you have no attachments then?'

'None,' he says, lip curling.

My voice is a whisper but the words come out sharp as a winter wind. 'Why are you here then? Why do you return to me? Why am I, a mere mortal, allowed to see you, speak to you...touch you?'

For a second he nods lightly. And then like a slap it strikes him across the face. Fear and fury flare his nostrils and in the flutter of a second, I realize what is about to happen. At last I have found the question that disturbs him more than the deaths of children.

The last thing I see is his fist uncurl.

And then I travel. For the longest time, the ground is torn from beneath my feet. Through dancing storms and raging sunshine, I swim backward and backward until –

I land.

I know where I am before I can open my eyes. I smell wet leaves, the soggy barks of trees and sweat clinging to human flesh. I feel the weight of a head in my lap, heavy like a melon.

*Dying is wish-fulfilment like no other.*

When I open my eyes I am there. Back on the forest floor, holding my husband's body limply to my chest. He awakens, clutching his chest, not quite like a man enjoying a song, and he looks at me, his eyes shining with something like reverence.

I sit there, numb. I am numb when he speaks to me. Numb when we return home. Numb when I gaze at my reflection in a pond and find a 15 year old's face frown back at me. It's as if my compass spins endlessly now, and north is lost or torn to pieces and scattered everywhere like ash and bone.

As the days pass, our village is rife with rumour. Nobody asks what I saw or where I went. Nobody understands the price of infuriating a god. 'Savitri haunted Death until he gave back her husband,' they say. 'She must have impressed the god with her sharp mind. She must have pleased Him with her devotion.'

I am not that Savitri. No.

I am a little girl, cold in the summer sun, holding on to a basket of sickeningly sweet fruit.

# ΛPOCΛLΥPTICΛ

## KRISHNΛ UDΛΥΛSΛNKΛR

There has to be another way.

There isn't. For the darkness to take over completely, not even a spark of light must remain. It is time to stain our hands with blood. Besides, what does it matter? If there is divinity left in this world, none of it has dwelt in me, from long before I sent that little girl into that room.

I watch as he studies her with unrestrained lust, a man five times her age. It is unavoidable, he constantly seeks my presence, invokes me twice a day into the many simulacra that he has around him — even in this, his room of pleasure and vice. I cannot deny that his devotion is absolute, for he thinks of me with his every breath; even now, as he prepares to rape this child, he thanks me for all that I have given him, including the power to buy this sin.

I wonder how it is that a man who thinks of me so often can bring himself to behave this way. What does that say about me?

It is a question I've asked myself often and, of late, all answers have led to this moment. There is no other way.

Vishnu disagrees with me – I don't blame him, it is in his nature to *manage*, to *sustain*, to *preserve*: All three words lofty, meaningless terms for a new kind of impotence fueled by faith in justice at the end of an unseen infinity. But millennia of pointing that out – thus disagreeing with him – has only earned me the title of being fickle, to the point he had a nickname for me.

'My darling Chanchala,' he would say, bundling me close to his muscular chest, well-assured that I would never leave him.

Will he understand what I plan to do now, once it has been done? I guess not, but I don't care. If all goes well, neither of us will be around to argue about it. It's why I had told him twice, this morning, that I love him. But he had just smiled his usual, beatific smile that drove the whole world mad, then turned on to his side and fallen asleep again on our plush waterbed. Soon, he will have no choice but to wake.

The girl screams at the sight of the advancing man; it is what her tormentor wants, what he has paid for. I tell her without words that she will not remember this horror, though *I* will for whatever time we both have left to us. As the man begins to undress in preparation for his evening of pleasure, I slip into the room, unnoticed, and take what it is I want, what this elaborate trap has been designed for. Once, I could have done it with a snap of my fingers and a bolt of thunder for added effect, if it were public. But the growing darkness diminishes me, and I am reduced to guile and deceit and, above all, to sacrifice what is not mine to sacrifice. Thankfully, I still have other – if only middling – powers left, and I make what use I can of them.

I walk out of the building and into the glare of headlights on Mumbai's Cuffe Parade. The over-speeding Mercedes blares its horn, slows down, then speeds up again, the driver wondering what it was that he just saw — or didn't see. I couldn't give a fuck, not right now. I continue crossing the road and enter the building on the other side. Manhattan's skyline gleams victorious as I ride up the elevator — they don't call them lifts here — to the 72nd floor.

It is night here too, on the other side of the world, a fact that could be, should be surprising if one stops to consider it. But these days, it is night everywhere, and all Surya and Soma can do about it is wring their hands before Brahma or blame Vishnu for not preserving the natural order of things.

When it came to that, Vishnu, in his typical diplomatic manner, always managed to soothe their fragile egos before retreating into his tortoise shell till he had calmed himself down. But the last time around, things had gotten bad, belligerent even. Surya had threatened to take the matter to Shiva. Vishnu had been so pissed that he nearly went Narasimha on us all before finally squeezing himself into his tortoise shell. He had taken three days to come home, instead of the usual one. I hadn't minded. That's when I'd had the idea, and I had used his absence to begin planning.

The elevator doors open with a smooth hiss, and I step out to find Vidya waiting.

She gives me a questioning look, though she knows the answer and is already making her way towards one of the high-security doors that lead out from the lobby. I join her and hold up the card key I have recently procured. The door opens, and we enter.

'You sure there's no one here?' It's my turn to be sceptical.

'Absolutely,' Vidya replies. 'Every single employee is in the conference room on the 13th floor. Without exception.'

'Nice,' I say, not without admiration. 'How did you manage that?'

'TED Talk. You know how it is. No one gives a damn about listening or learning anything, but everyone wants be seen at one anyway. I tried doing free tickets to the premiere of a Tom Cruise movie but half of them didn't seem to care. A TED Talk, on the other hand…'

Trust Vidya to come up with the smartest plan. But then, as she had pointed out the other day: 'I am, by definition, the most intelligent being in the universe. But you know what that counts for these days? Zilch.'

I had argued, 'Well, EQ matters as much as IQ.'

'EQ and IQ be damned, Lakshmi. Intelligence and knowledge are supposed to lead to success. But that formula worked only as long as compassion and kindness were of any worth. These days, the definition works in reverse: success is being rich, powerful, unstoppable, and whatever makes you rich, powerful and unstoppable is seen as intelligence. That it took me so long to see it should tell you how dumb I am, by current standards.'

'You're still smart enough to help me do the right thing, Vidya,' I had told her, outlining my plan. It had taken her barely a moment to figure it all out; she had not needed any convincing.

I had suggested, 'So…maybe fire a few nuclear missiles? Or as many as there exist in the world? Should do the job quickly, right?'

Vidya had scoffed. 'It's only in the movies that you can hack into some place and launch a missile by remote control. In reality, the launch protocols are very, very physical. The 'launch codes' you hear so much about are really just codes to open a safe or similar physical space from which you'd need to take a physical key and insert it into something to launch a rocket. Even the guidance systems for something like the ICBs – intercontinental ballistic missiles – are not online, they are preset on stand-alone computers. No, it can't be the missiles. We'll have to figure out another way. There are plenty.'

She had gone on to talk about backdoors installed in nearly every major software used by corporations and governments alike, and explained how these would let her do an array of things: from turning satellites and disabling security systems to setting off military coups, multinational conglomerate-sponsored coups, and every other kind of overthrow that one could think of, as well as to cause nearly every automated function on the planet – from remote-controlled garage doors to life-support systems – to go bonkers.

'On the environmental side,' she had continued, 'I can change configurations to alter resource exploration parameters and mining plans...'

'In Sanskrit, please,' I had interrupted, 'Or any other intelligible language of your choice.'

Vidya had grinned; even in that situation, her innate dark humour had reared its head. 'Big shiny satellite takes photo from outer space. Super-intelligent software looks at photo and identifies possible oil fields, mineral deposits, and so on. Software sends coordinates to gigantic, mean drilling machine that can go right into the planet's core, telling it where to dig. Me bad girl. Me hack into software to give it new parameters. Software tells mean machine to dig in dangerous, very dangerous, places.'

She had then dropped her attempt at being simplistically funny and continued in her normal tone, 'Take this fault line,' she had pointed at a circle with an X she had marked up on the cloud she had been using for a whiteboard. 'If you cut through here, it should trigger an earthquake that has an epicentre here, which means both sides of the Pacific would pretty much collapse into the ocean, and what's left of the world would be wiped out by the resulting tsunami. Add to that the fact that I will speed up the melting of the polar ice caps...'

'Any safe place left?' I had asked. I had not meant to be sarcastic, only thorough.

Vidya had pointed to the small tract of land that would, she explained, remained untouched for a few hours, till changing global temperatures and rising ocean levels took care of that too. 'Which means...'

'Which means we need help. And that help we shall have.'

'Do you think she will...?'

'Do you doubt her courage?' We both had known the question was rhetorical.

'Of course not,' Vidya had replied. 'But he...he is strong.'

'He is her equal. No more, no less. And now, more than ever, is when that will matter. But let's get your end of things sorted out first before we loop her in. How long will it all take?'

Vidya had said, 'The problem with hacking from one system into another is that you need to spread out the impact, so that no one really sees it for what it is. To do that can take years... centuries, if you let the species evolve to survive.'

'And for a clean slate?'

Vidya had frowned as she did some calculations in her head. 'It can be done. I can collapse things together to maximize the domino effect. It'll be bloody and take some mayhem. I can tweak the signaling systems to mass transports in all the world's major cities, and the airports too. High-speed trains, planes, cars — the largest number of accidents in the smallest possible time. Once that is done, shut down all the power and other infrastructure. Riots will start in moments. Of course, rural areas will remain relatively peaceful for longer, but I can work region by region — open up all the dams, trigger any nuclear reactions there may be, et cetera, et cetera. But...'

'But...?'

'To do all this in a short time frame, I need a hard entry. Some system that I can manually log into to gain access to all the world's computers and data systems. From there, I can hack into the rest.'

'Hard entry? Like a physical key or login and password?'

'Yes, usually a little more complicated, like a high-security device of some sort.'

'I'll take care of that. Tell me what you need.'

Vidya had looked over the cloud before zeroing in on the exact point.

'There. This guy. He's a trader on the Mumbai Stock Exchange, if you can call him that without insulting traders in general. A criminal through and through, but rich enough to pass off as a decent businessman. His office system connects to a server we can use. I'll need his security card key. I'll need his fingerprints too, but we can still weave that ourselves, I think...'

There was nothing I could say to that. We could only hope that our powers would still let us do that much. As far as electronics and technology went, our divinity had ceased to affect these things a long time ago.

'And once you get it? How long...'

'Less than 24 hours,' she had replied.

And so, I had arranged for the card key, which Vidya now waves in front of a reader that she has hooked up to one of the computers here in this New York law firm. I watch as she types furiously, line after line of code that somehow makes sense to me, though it should not. I see the power outages and the fires, the psychosis and mass murders, the misery and death she is programming into place. Terrible as it seems, I remind myself that it is nothing that is not already happening, or will not happen for ages to come. But, if we act, we restrict the suffering to the lifetimes of those living in the universe right now. And theirs will, if all goes well, be a very short lifetime indeed.

Vidya's slim fingers hover over the keyboard, curled as though she is about to strike a chord on her favourite veenai. She looks at me – not that she needs my permission, but more so because she wants me to enjoy this moment as much as she will. And we will both dread it as much as we enjoy it.

I nod. She smiles and hits enter, looking at the reaction her code causes on the many other computer screens that have been set to scroll information of all sorts from around the world.

'She is free,' she says.

Bhoomi, dear sister, the patient, all-enduring one. We should have protested when they began caging her with their undersea cables and deep-water drills, their high-rise buildings on reclaimed sea and covered-up lakes and heavy overland bridges – all built with sand and soil from life-giving riverbeds. But we had not, partly because she would smile and tell us it was all for her children, and so it was all right. We should never have agreed to that. We should never have agreed to many things; no matter the explanations of 'natural course' and 'universal balance' and 'good must equal bad' and all that crap. We should have told her straight: 'They call you "mother" and then fuck you over. What does that make them?'

It's time she gives those motherfuckers what they deserve.

Maybe that is universal balance at work, after all. Frankly, I don't care. I also don't care that I am saying it a few times too many.

'Did you feel that?' Vidya asks me.

I have. It was too low on the Richter scale for anything but sensitive instruments to pick up, and I guess we are both sensitive instruments enough — at least as far as nature is concerned. 'I guess that was about a 2 or 3. Yup, she's free all right. Watch out for the big ones.'

'This should speed things up,' Vidya says, throwing her arms up in a stretch. She gives me a look of satisfied finality and stands up. 'Job done. We have about an hour before power goes out world over. Is there anywhere you want to be?'

I hesitate for the first time since we began all this. Being who I am, what I am, I've always known this day would come, when I'd watch all of Creation collapse into the nothingness it had come from. I would be one of the last to go, but I would go too, and that thought has as yet never filled me with regret. Indeed, there had been an unspeakable intimacy, a lump-in-the-throat warmth at the thought of standing next to Vishnu, our shoulders touching, our fingers intertwined. And then, I supposed, I would turn, as would he, so that we looked into each other's eyes. The last thing we would see in this form and existence would be each other.

'Yes,' I tell her. 'I should get going. There isn't much time.'
'Me too.'

Vidya draws me into a hug; it is cheerful somehow, not desperate or sad or pained. I want to ask her if she means to go spend what time is left with Brahma, but decide not to. Theirs has been a complicated relationship, some say inappropriate. I've never had a comment to make on that, but I have always thought of her as far too intelligent for that old-fashioned creator anyway.

'See you...or not!' she says and begins making her way to the door. She has a spring in her step that makes me think that wherever she is headed to, it is some place she loves and is always happy in.

I soak in her joy for a borrowed moment, before returning to what I must do.

I take the elevator back downstairs and out of the building. Looking up, I can see people beginning to cluster at the floor-to-ceiling windows of the conference room, marveling — or is it despairing — at something on the skyline. Clearly, their TED Talk just got way too real.

I cross the road over to Mumbai and take the lift back up to the den of decadence that I had left barely a few moment ago. I slip in as I had slipped out, to find the trader stroking himself to preparedness in front of the TV, a lit cigarette dangling dangerously from the fingers of his other hand. His drink, a large shot of neat whisky, has already been knocked over, the liquid slowly dripping off the table to form a pool barely inches away from where the still-glowing cigarette ash has burned a hole in the carpet. He does not notice, intent as he is on the pornography he is watching as he waits for his booze-fuelled Viagra to kick in.

I smile. Perhaps there is balance left in this world. Perhaps, there is a purpose to divinity, after all. Even though it no longer holds purpose for me.

I walk into the bedroom and shut the door behind me, just as the carpet bursts into flames, along with the man occupying it. His screams begin but I wave my hand to mute them out.

I turn to the girl. She has seen enough horrors for one night – no, for a lifetime. She watches me – an unlikely figure in that place – in fear, straining against her bonds. I smile at her, she sees much behind the gesture and stops resisting. Going up to her, I undo the bindings on her arms and then hold her against me. She curls up like the child she is and begins to cry in relief. I place a hand on her head, it soothes her; it also makes her impervious to the pain that will follow. She will feel my warmth as I bundle her closer still, but not the searing heat that now hits my back.

It does not have to end this way; I don't have to end this way. But something tells me it should.

The flames dance over my skin. I begin to scream.

## II.

You should be angry. And you don't disappoint. Always, they would send me to calm you down, do a little shimmy, maybe a lap dance, till your rage gave way to other emotions. Then they would leave, the wise and the demigods, the celestials and the humans, all with knowing smiles on their faces, almost like mental high-fives because hey, their buddy, their gang leader is going to score tonight.

This time, the joke is on you.

They say when your anger breaches the bounds of your supposedly impeccable self-control, your third eye will open and the world will come to an end. Now, it is the end of the world that has stoked your wrath. Go ahead, open your third eye, burn all that you see.

Begin with me.

Hurry up. That little crack? That was Africa splitting apart. Those cries you hear? They're drowning in Chennai, in your little bastion of *vibuthi* and insentient stone phalluses; can you hear them? But you didn't hear it when, in that same city, a girl screamed her head off in broad daylight on a railway station platform as someone hacked her to death with a sickle, did you? This world has already been destroyed a thousand times over in just the last second. It crumbles to meaningless dust whenever a god turns away.

The beginning of the beginning, they called you; there was no room for me there. It took a pseudo-feminist revolution for you to admit I was your equal half, no me without you, no you without me. Two things for your kind attention, you self-absorbed p… Hey, I was going to say phallus again. That's neither offensive nor inaccurate, is it? So, sit on your bull and listen.

Number one: you don't get to give me anything. Not equality, not status as your half. I take what is mine, so stuff your condescension high up the Himalayas. And, please, I wasn't born in the last yuga for you to try that, 'I'm saving the world by having a mistress,' shit. My problem with Ganga wasn't that she was competition to me, as you'd want the world to believe. My problem with her was that she never resisted, never fought back. And I…I was just like her. I never fought back either, not against you, not against anyone. And so I hated her, because I didn't dare hate myself.

What good does it serve the world when the Mother of All despises herself for being a spineless wimp? Turns out, not hating myself hasn't turned out all that well either.

Look, that's North America going up in flames.

Number two: there was a Me without you. A Me you could not handle. A Me that brought life into this world, with my sweat and turmeric and the fragrance of pure love – maternal love, you m… Never mind.

And what did you do? You killed him. Killed him, then brought him back to life with the head of an elephant. And then, only then did you call him our son, because now it had your benevolence written all over it, didn't it?

It was always about you. And the worst part – you made it seem that it was about right and wrong, justice and order. Like with my dad.

So, he was an asshole, an abusive control freak. And you called him out on it. But you couldn't just do that as a friend and spouse and nice guy, could you. No, it had to be all about how I was your wife and no longer his daughter, and what it meant to be devoted to you and blah blah blah. And then you go do the whole 'I am under my wife's foot' shenanigans – not to mention that you made me out to be a bitch there. Durga, Kali… Whatever gave you the idea that I'd want anyone, anyone whosoever, under my foot, enslaved and subjugated in a mock-demonstration to the world of your piddling equality? Says much for what you think of godliness and power, don't you? Oh, I could crush you underfoot because that is true power but look how nice I am, I don't.

I never needed you underfoot. Nor did I need you to lift me up. I am what I am, as we all are. And, really, you should have thought of all that before you went ahead and killed my son. You're not very bright as gods go, are you?

And that deafening silence, my dear husband, was Europe, suffocating under ash. Your favourite condiment. Or is it accoutrement, I'm not sure which, really. I guess, I don't care; not about you, not anymore.

You like being called the Destroyer, the end of all ends, don't you? Go ahead, end it now.

It's you and me. And the world ends all the same.

How romantic.

## III.

Vidya hummed an indistinct tune as she walked the two blocks from the office building to the midtown branch of the New York Public Library, beginning with the Raga Abheri, then moving to Pink Floyd before letting Eminem keep pace with her brisk footsteps. It was, she knew, well after library hours, but that did not stop her as she let herself into the older structure nestled amongst the many high-rises of Fifth Avenue, including the Empire State Building. She had always loved this place, loved it even before it had been built on, as though the very soil of that spot had sung to her, asked her to lay down with her back against its cool petrichor till she and it were one. Of all the places that reminded her of what it was to be who she was, this was the closest and, admittedly, her favourite.

If someone had asked her, she would have said it was the beauty in the irony of it all: A breathtakingly realistic renaissance-style mural of a cloud-smattered sky painted against a plastered ceiling. Skylights set into a lofty arched roof that was nevertheless dwarfed by the high-rises around them. Gilded rosettes and elaborate woodworks that were a pain to dust by the day. And, of course, the smell of books, the feeling of knowledge bubbling, electrifying, as she rested her fingertips against the polished reading desks, each with their individual lamps.

The reading room was empty at this hour, but for some reason the lights remained, without her intervention, physical or otherwise, switched on. A warm glow surrounded every desk, each table cocooned in its golden circle of light. One could be surrounded by people here and yet be wonderfully alone. And one could be alone and yet be surrounded by the best company.

Vidya breathed in deep. Despite the air-conditioning, the library had the same, lovely smell of books as a second-hand bookstore on College Street in Kolkata or a family-run home library in a village in Croatia. Paper, parchment, silk, stone… She had seen it in every form and the smell remained the same. It always made her happy. Often, it had kept her alive, to the extent that living and dying had been options available to gods.

A flicker, then a distant explosion, and all the lights in the building went out. Vidya smiled to herself in the darkness and made her way, slowly, into the stacks of books around the space. She sat down on the ground, her back to the shelves, the sense of books against her spine, as though they now held her up. She did not know how long she had been sitting there before the noise began – a distant murmur that soon grew to a rolling rumble – the noise of a crowd, no, a mob, an angry mob. Yes, it would not be long now. With the world plunged into darkness and chaos, people in the vicinity would soon search for the means of making light.

Humans were, that way, extremely intelligent and resourceful. It was their quest for knowledge that Vidya had found delightful and remarkable; their overwhelming urge to comprehend even the incomprehensible, to measure the universe and span the cosmos, to identify the very gods. She did not understand when and how it had begun to go wrong; or, wait, perhaps she did.

Knowledge had brought power. Somewhere, somehow, power had begun to matter more. What use in understanding power when you could wield it instead? What use in understanding divinity when you could become gods instead? If only the humans had understood that they were gods, or had been, and would have remained so if they had tempered their knowledge with compassion, their power with kindness.

Big bullshit words.

*Where did I go wrong?*

Vidya sighed, the sound lost in a loud crash as one of the large, arched windows was broken through and a crowd began to pour into the library. At first, unthinking hands reached out for whatever they could lay their hands on. Then the mob took on a brief semblance of order as it remembered why it was there. Few things were more flammable – or incendiary – than books.

The scourge began; people first took a book or two, then realized that they could carry more, and more meant power, it meant trade and domination, not just in the moment but in the future, when all sources of fuel ran out; perhaps they could be kings – no, gods – in the dark times ahead. But there would be no future, nothing beyond a brief and thorough end of the present.

The din grew louder as fights began to break out. The mob's mind moved from taking for itself to making sure that others had less. Books were thrown about and torn, before human efficiency prevailed: someone brought out a lighter. A pile of books began to glow, then crackle, the golden blaze spreading to the tables and walls till it reached the very stack Vidya leant against. She smiled and shut her eyes against the inferno that would destroy all Creation.

Next time, she hoped, humanity would be what it was meant to be. Next time, she prayed, the gods would get it right.

# LIST OF CONTRIBUTORS

**Asma Kazi** is a mixed media artist. Her art is carnivalesque, influenced by pop culture, the chaos theory, biomorphism and inspirations drawn from following the breadcrumb trail of the enchanted every day. She has worked as an artist professionally since 2012. Her artwork currently resides with collectors around the world. Some of her commercial art projects include artwork created for Joseph Gordon-Levitt, Hachette Books and Zee TV. 'Bahameen' is her first short story. Asma can be contacted at her website www.kaleidodrama.com and on Twitter @a5ma.

**Kiran Manral** is a novelist and TEDx speaker whose work spans many genres. Her latest book is the psychological thriller, *Missing: Presumed Dead*. Her other works include *The Reluctant Detective, Once upon a Crush, All Aboard, Saving Maya, The Face at the Window* (2016) *True Love Stories, Karmic Kids* and *A Boy's Guide to Growing Up*. The Indian Council of UN Relations (ICUNR) awarded her the International Women's Day Award 2018 for excellence in the field of writing.

**Krishna Udayasankar** is the author of the bestselling Aryavarta Chronicles series (*Govinda, Kaurava* and *Kurukshetra*), *Immortal* and *3* – a novel based on the founding myth of Singapore. She is also the author of *Objects of Affection*, a full-length collection of prose poems and the co-editor of *Body Boundaries: The Etiquette Anthology of Women's Writing*. Her next book is the fantasy novel *Beast*. Krishna tweets @krisudayasankar.

**Nikita Deshpande** graduated from St. Xavier's College, Mumbai, where she read English literature, and was the recipient of a scholarship at Vermont Studio Center. She has assisted directors on prominent films such as *Fukrey* and *Mirzya*, and was the screenwriter/director of the commercial that won Crash the Pepsi IPL in 2015. Her debut novel, *It Must've Been Something He Wrote*, was published in 2016. Nikita lives in Mumbai, where she hoards stationery and competes with her partner every day to see who makes the perfect cup of filter *kaapi*. Nikita tweets @deepblueruin.

**Ruchika Roy** is an award-winning screenwriter with more than 12 years of experience in the world of television and movies. She also ran a tattoo studio called Funky Monkey and then later headed the creative team of an event company. She has written short features for the *Observer* as well as *Thought Catalog*. Her latest professional stint was as creative director/senior executive producer for a leading digital content platform. Currently she is involved with writing web shows about psychopaths and adventurers. 'The Gatekeeper's Intern' is her first short story. Ruchika tweets @roysrus.

**Samhita Arni** started writing and illustrating her first book when she was eight. The book, *The Mahabharata: A Child's View*, went on to sell 50,000 copies worldwide. Her second book, *Sita's Ramayana*, a graphic novel, was on the *New York Times* bestseller list for graphic novels for two weeks. She is the author of the novel *The Missing Queen* and her latest novel is *The Prince*. Samhita tweets @samarni and you can contact her at sam@samarni.com.

Sejal Mehta is a writer, editor and content consultant. An old travel hack, she has worked with Marine Life of Mumbai, *Lonely Planet Magazine India*, *National Geographic Traveller India*, *Nature inFocus* and *Saevus Wildlife*. Previously, she has also worked with J.P. Morgan and *Femina*, and contributed to *Scroll*, *Indian Express*, *Mint*, *BBC Top Gear*, *BBC Knowledge*, *DNA*, *Free Press Journal*, *Mongabay*, *Times of India* and *Hindustan Times*. She is a published author for children's books. Find Sejal on Twitter @sejalmehta06.

Shreya Ila Anasuya is a writer of fiction and non-fiction, an independent journalist, and the managing editor of *Skin Stories*, an award-winning publication on sexuality, disability and gender, housed at the non-profit Point of View. Shreya is the recipient of three Laadli Media Awards and a Toto Award for Creative Writing in English. Shreya is working on their debut book and lives in Mumbai with a cat called Begum. Shreya can be contacted on www.shreyailaanasuya.com.

Shveta Thakrar is a part-time nagini and full-time believer in magic. Her work has appeared in a number of magazines and anthologies including *Enchanted Living*, *Uncanny Magazine*, *A Thousand Beginnings and Endings* and *Toil & Trouble*. Her debut young adult fantasy novel, *Star Daughter*, is forthcoming. When not spinning stories, Shveta crafts, devours books, daydreams, travels, bakes and occasionally even plays her harp. Find Shveta at shvetathakrar.com or on Twitter @ShvetaThakrar.

Shweta Taneja is a bestselling Indian fantasy and science fiction author, best known for her fantasy series, Anantya Tantrist Mysteries. She's a Charles Wallace India fellow and was awarded the Best Asian Speculative Fiction Editor's Choice

Award for her short story 'The Daughter That Bleeds'. Her graphic novel *Krishna: Defender of Dharma* is in the must-read lists of government schools in India. Shweta can be found most places online with her handle @shwetawrites.

Sukanya Venkatraghavan is the author of the fantasy novel *Dark Things*. She started her film journalism career with *Filmfare* and was also the entertainment editor at *Marie Claire*. Sukanya has been part of the creative team, including scripting and research, for shows such as *Look Who's Talking With Niranjan* (ZEE Café), *Design HQ* Season 2 (Fox Life) and *Koffee with Karan* (Season 6). She is currently working on her next book. Sukanya tweets @suku06.

S.V. Sujatha was born in Chennai, the land of filter coffee, elaborate meals and wonderful temples. She is a graduate of the Warwick Writing Programme. She likes writing fiction, especially of the speculative kind, because she finds real life boring and cruel. Her last outing, *The Demon Hunter of Chottanikkara* was born out of her love for the Mother Goddess and passion for Indian mythology. Sujatha tweets @Sujatha_sv.

Tashan Mehta is a novelist based in Mumbai. She graduated from the universities of Warwick and Cambridge, where she first developed her interests in form and the fantastical. Her debut novel, *The Liar's Weave*, was published in the Indian subcontinent in 2017 and has been shortlisted for the inaugural Prabha Khaitan Woman's Voice Award. She has been part of the Sangam House International Writers' Residency and was selected to be the British Council writer-in-residence at Anglia Ruskin University, UK. She is currently working on her second and third novels. Contact her at tashanmehta.com.

Trisha Das is the author of *Draupadi Kuru: After the Pandavas*, *The Mahabharata Re-imagined*, *The Art of the Television Interview* and the internationally acclaimed *How to Write a Documentary Script*. She has written and directed over 40 documentaries in her filmmaking career. Trisha has also won an Indian National Film Award (2005) and was UGA's 'International Artist of the Year' (2003). Her latest novel is *Kama's Last Sutra*. Trisha tweets @thetrishadas.

# ΛCKNOWLEDGEMENTS

A book that started as a dream now ends with immense gratitude. Curating and editing *Magical Women* has been a little like making a multi-star blockbuster. It has had action, drama and lots of emotion, and in the end it has turned out to be exactly what I hoped it would be – a beautiful book of stories teeming with estrogen magic.

I must begin with my coven of authors. You have my heart forever for placing your faith in a one-book-old writer with a mad dream about a speculative fiction anthology. Thank you for your enthusiasm, the stories, and letting me learn from you.

Magical women all over the universe, this book exists because you do.

Thank you, Samit Basu, possibly the first person I mentioned this dream project to. I could not have done this without your support, guidance and kindness. Krishna Udayasankar for being a rock through this whole process. They say writers shouldn't be friends but what do they know. Sharanya Manivannan for the love you have shown this book and me. Vidya Balan, for your kind words of encouragement, thank you always.

Poulomi Chatterjee, for all the whiny phone calls that end up in giggles, for your steadfast vision and guidance, and ultimately for the faith you've had in this book and me. Prerna Vohra for backing me and making this book happen. Sini Nair, expert handler of contracts, multiple email threads and grumpy authors, you are amazing. Ansila Thomas and Niyati Dhuldhoya for being wonderful editorial pillars of support. Asma Kazi, for the breathtaking cover illustration and Bhavi Mehta for the design. The entire team at Hachette India for every little and big acts of assistance throughout this process.

Family, friends who let me grump all over you during the last one and a half years and cheered me on constantly. My husband, Venkat, without whom none of my dreams would come true.

And finally, you, lovely reader – *Magical Women* is in the right hands now and I am glad you guys met.

Sukanya Venkatraghavan

ALSO AVAILABLE FROM HACHETTE INDIA

The Gollancz Book of South Asian Science Fiction

*Edited by Tarun K. Saint*

ISBN 9789388322058
HARDBACK
Rs 599

Singular visions of the future that will thrill, amuse,
startle and intrigue

On an ordinary morning, the citizens of Karachi wake up to discover
the sea missing from their shores. The last Parsi left on Earth
must look for other worlds to escape to when debt collectors come
knocking. A family visiting a Partition-themed park gets more
entertainment than they bargained for. Gandhi appears in the present
day under rather unusual circumstances. Aliens with an agenda arrive
at a railway station in Uttar Pradesh. Two young scientists seek
to communicate with forests even as the web of life threatens to
collapse. A young girl's personal tragedy finds a surprising resolution
as she readies herself for an expedition of a lifetime.

These and other tales of masterful imagination illuminate this
essential volume of new science fiction that brings together some
of the most creative minds in contemporary literature. A must-have
collectible, The Gollancz Book of South Asian Science Fiction
offers fresh perspectives on our hyper-global, often alienating and
always paranoid world, in which humanity and love may yet triumph.

Featuring the works of: Adrish Bardhan * Arunava Sinha * Harishankar
Parsai * C.M. Naim * Asif Farrukhi * Syed Saeed Naqvi* Somendra
Singh Kharola * Mimi Mondal * Rahul Sankrityayan * Maya Joshi
* Anil Menon * Shovon Chowdhury * Kaiser Haq *Sumita Sharma
*Tarun K. Saint * Priya Sarukkai Chabria * Suraj Prasad * Manjula
Padmanabhan * Payal Dhar * Sami Ahmad Khan * Premendra
Mitra * Arjun Rajendran * Chandrashekhar Sastry * Giti Chandra
* Mohammad Salman * Rimi B. Chatterjee * Muhammed Zafar Iqbal
* Rukmini Bhaya Nair * Nur Nasreen Ibrahim * Keki N. Daruwalla
* S.B. Divya *Vandana Singh